The Gondolier and the Russian Countess

David Ruffle

Paperback ISBN 978-1-78092-945-3
ePub ISBN 978-1-78092-946-0
PDF ISBN 978-1-78092-947-7

Published in the UK by MX Publishing
335 Princess Park Manor, Royal Drive,
London, N11 3GX
www.mxpublishing.co.uk

Cover design by www.staunch.com

Also by David Ruffle

Sherlock Holmes and the Lyme Regis Horror
Sherlock Holmes and the Lyme Regis Horror (expanded 2nd Edition)
Sherlock Holmes and the Lyme Regis Legacy
Holmes and Watson: End Peace
Sherlock Holmes and the Lyme Regis Trials
The Abyss (A Journey with Jack the Ripper)
A Twist of Lyme
Sherlock Holmes: The Lyme Regis Trilogy (Illustrated Omnibus Edition)
Another Twist of Lyme
A Further Twist of Lyme
Holmes and Watson: An American Adventure
Holmes and Watson: An Evening in Baker Street
Sherlock Holmes and the Scarborough Affair (with Gill Stammers)

For Children
Sherlock Holmes and the Missing Snowman (illustrated by Rikey Austin)

As editor and contributor
Tales from the Stranger's Room (Vol. 1)
Tales from the Stranger's Room (Vol. 2)

For Gill

......with memories of Venice.

Preamble

A question: What connects Venice to Laurel and Hardy? No? Let me explain.

A few years ago on the Holmesian.net website I offered up for general consumption a short piece wherein Holmes and Watson meet Stan and Ollie. Bizarre, I know. But I get these ideas sometimes. I tend to think that if you keep Holmes and Watson firmly grounded in character then all manner of things can happen around them...but it still works. All in the eye of the beholder. Or the writer.

Anyway, at the start of this small piece, I had Watson attempting to write up from his notes the affair of *The Gondolier and the Russian Countess*. It was suggested by a couple of folk from that now defunct website that although the Laurel and Hardy piece was interesting in a light, fluffy and certainly bizarre way (see, told you it was bizarre) it might be far more interesting to actually read about the said gondolier and the Russian bird.

Several years later; here it is. And if you are good and read it all, you can visit Stan and Ollie later.

A note: The action takes place in 1902 and exists in the little universe I created for the Holmes/Lyme Regis trilogy. This comes after *Horror* and *Legacy*, but before *Trials*. So, Watson is married to Beatrice, who we don't encounter here for she is once more in Lyme Regis. None of which will make any sense if you have not read any of that trilogy. But, you can. If you wish.

David Ruffle Lyme Regis 2016.

'That title, c'mon now.'
'What about it?'
'You gotta change it, mate.'
'No way, I like it. What's wrong with it anyway?'
'The Gondolier and the Russian Countess! People will mistake it for a Mills and Boon. They'll think they have a romance on their hands; love across the social divide, how love conquers all, my nights with my sexy gondolier...'
'If these people have read my books before they will know not to expect a love story.'
'Don't be too sure, kid. You are far too fond of a little romance. Just change the title, be a sport.'
'To what? Let's hear your ideas.'
'Nice, easy and direct. Does what it says on the cover. How about Death in Venice?'
'Been done.'
'Or one which has Holmes and Watson in constant fear of being followed; Don't Look Now."'
'Du Maurier beat me to it!'
'Did he?'
'She.'
'Okay, okay keep the title, but none of this finding Watson's papers underneath your grandmother's bed or his dispatch-box being found by children on an Easter Egg hunt in the wilds of Surrey. Keep it real, mate.'
'But it's not really real is it, not really.'
'Look, I know it's not really real, but some people out there think Sherlock Holmes was an actual living person.'
'Idiots.'
'They might be, but they are part of your target audience.'
'Okay, so no provenance, but keep it real. And I get to keep the title, yes?'
'If you must.'

Chapter One

The year 1902 was a particularly busy one for Sherlock Holmes and needless to say, a triumphant one. He basked in the glory that his many successes brought him and his doings became a fixture in the national press, not just in this country, but the length and breadth of Europe. He was consulted on various matters by several ruling heads on the continent; some of these he looked into, some he deemed not worthy of his time however distinguished the client may have been. The puzzles that were presented to him, if sufficiently intriguing, were more important to him than the status of those who presented such problems. Some of the cases from that year have already found their way into my chronicles, but some will never appear before the public because their publication would do irreparable harm to those closely associated with them. As always, I have to exercise a certain amount of discretion in my selection of which tales to lay before the public.

In the autumn of 1902 Holmes had been consulted by none other than His Holiness the Pope regarding certain criminal factions at work in the Vatican. This matter called for the utmost discretion for it was decreed by the Pontiff that it must never be made public. Such was his faith in Holmes that he never once entertained the notion that he would fail to bring the culprits to book.

I had accompanied Holmes to Rome as he seemed desirous of my presence and if I could not always be of any material use I reckoned I could indulge myself in visiting the antiquities of that famed city. My dear wife was more than happy with this arrangement. Beatrice herself was spending the autumn in Lyme Regis with her son, Nathaniel and his wife, Elizabeth.

Despite the shadowy figures who manipulated the inner politics of the Vatican, who were determined to prevent Holmes from arriving at the truth, he nevertheless brought the matter to a successful conclusion securing the undying admiration of Pope Leo VIII. His Holiness, before we took our leave, led us down one of the Vatican's many corridors to the Sistine Chapel. There, we wandered at will, in deep appreciation of Michelangelo's magnificent artistry. I don't believe I have ever been in so much awe of something in my life. Words cannot do justice to what I saw that day, save to say that it was an almost spiritual moment for me.

Cardinal Roselli, the Pontiff's right-hand man during Holmes's investigation was now undertaking a journey to Venice which had been postponed while these grave matters were resolved. He extended an invitation for us to travel with him. I was enthusiastic for it was a city I had always wanted to see although I had planned to visit Beatrice in Lyme on my immediate return from Rome. He had never mentioned it until that moment, but it seems Holmes was familiar with Venice, it apparently was his next port of call after departing Florence during his years 'away'. However, after his busy year, he pronounced he was more than happy to spend some time there with me.

I wired Beatrice and her reply was to the effect that I must go on to Venice, it being too good an opportunity to miss. Her only proviso being that one day I would take her. This I agreed to gladly in my return wire.

The train tickets were most generously purchased utilising the Vatican funds and Pope Leo, in spite of his frailty, saw us off in person. Even as the train pulled out of the station, we could still see him standing there, one hand raised in acknowledgment, the other curled around an assistant's arm for support.

'The Holy Father is a man most impressive, *si signors*?'

'Indeed, he can look back on a long and honourable life,' replied Holmes.

'How old is he, may I ask?'

'He is ninety-two, *dottori*. Frail, but unbowed. Weak, but unbeaten. Now, do you need my help with securing accommodation in Venice? I have a few contacts.'

'That is very kind of you, Cardinal but we cannot impinge further on your kindness. I am sure we can find ourselves comfortable quarters, it is not the busiest time for Venice after all.'

'You will find it rather damp and the fog may not lift at all.'

'We are used to London peculiars, a most singular type of fog so I imagine we will cope with the Venice equivalent,' I remarked.

'Do not be too confident, Venice can surprise and delight in equal measure and the surprises are not always pleasant,' Roselli stated. 'I am familiar with your London fogs, my university days were spent there, but Venice fogs...well, you will see.'

'Myself and Watson are well-schooled in unpleasant surprises, be they meteorological or man-made. Hopefully, Venice will not provide instances of either.'

'I admire your confidence, *signor*. If you will excuse me, I need to bury my head in these papers,' the cardinal said, pulling some documents out of his satchel. 'The conference I am attending in Venice is convening to discuss ecumenical matters surrounding the education of creation in our schools and I need to reacquaint myself with the latest thinking on the matter. I never seem to have the time to delve deeply into current topics within the church and Cardinal Tosca who is acting as chairman can be quite hard on those that he thinks have not done sufficient homework.'

'Please go ahead, Cardinal. We will endeavour not to disturb you.'

The fact of whether we disturbed Cardinal Roselli or not was made largely redundant by the cardinal falling sound asleep after barely reading a page of his material. He bestirred himself only as the train drew into Venice *Santa Lucia* railway station.

'Did you have to put in the bit about Beatrice and Lyme Regis?'

'Yep, problem?'

'Who the hell is going to know who she is? Or where Lyme Regis is for that matter.'

'If they have read the Lyme Regis trilogy they will.'

'A big if, mate.'

'If they haven't, then perhaps this might encourage them.'

'A big perhaps. Look, I'm all for you selling more books, but we are keeping it real remember. Just saying that's all. Does the pope appear again?'

'You'll have to wait and see.'

'Smart-ass. And Roselli?'

'I refer you to my previous answer. Do I sense another problem looming?'

'Only if you waste time on characters who play no part in the story.'

'I might be just setting the scene.'

'Perhaps the readers might prefer that you get down to it with your Russian countess and her gondolier doing whatever countesses and gondoliers do!'

'I'll bear it in mind.'

Chapter Two

The Venice I'd encountered in picture-books, periodicals, journals and the like was not quite the Venice I encountered that day after coming out of the station and finding myself face to face with the Grand Canal. The air was damp and the city clothed in a thick fog which was almost impenetrable. The little I could see still managed to give me a sense of awe, much like the Sistine chapel ceiling had.

Holmes clapped me on the shoulder. 'Do not despair, Watson. The fog will lift sooner rather than later and the serene city will reveal itself to you.'

'Well, gentlemen I will leave you to the tender mercies of Venice. I trust the city will repay you well.'

'Thank you, Cardinal Roselli. We wish you success with your conference and hope that Cardinal Tosca is not too hard on you. Goodbye and thank you for your company and please pass on our best wishes to the Holy Father on your return to Rome.'

Several urchins approached us, jostling each other in their haste to carry our bags to our destination which was in any case as yet unknown. Our repeated '*non*' appeared not to dampen their enthusiasm for the task and I had to prise curled fingers from my valise's handle on several occasions until a coin sent spinning from Holmes's hand scattered them.

'On the whole, Watson, they are good boys who after all are only trying to earn a crust. There are some though who would gladly take your bag, but the ultimate destination of your bags would be very different from the one specified.'

'Do the police not interfere and arrest the culprits?'

'Arrest one and another will take his place. It is the way of the world here. The *polizia locale* have been known to turn a blind eye. Every so often to appease the city mayor there will be a roundup of suspects and a few token punishments handed out, but nothing really changes. I have a mind to search out lodgings on the *Via Garibaldi*, it is a little quieter there.'

'Whatever you say, Holmes, you are familiar with the city after all.'

'I have to warn you, Watson, that it is quite a fair step from here and it may be even longer if I cannot recall the shortcuts of eleven years ago.'

I followed Holmes through narrow alleys, down narrow streets, across bridges. I was convinced at times that we had doubled back on ourselves for some streets and alleys seemed familiar to me although the thick fog which hung in the air may have had something to do with my confusion. The mist had just begun to dissipate when we eventually entered a large square, much bigger than those five or six we had traversed.

'Do you recognise it?' asked Holmes.

'This must be St Mark's Square, Holmes. I recognise the basilica from photographs I have seen.'

'Quite so. Another ten minutes and we will be at our destination. Best foot forward. Don't dawdle, Watson, there will be time enough for sight-seeing.'

We walked along a wide promenade next to the lagoon where gondolas moored in rows bobbed up and down, the hulls splashing the surface. There was no slackening of pace from Holmes, but mercifully after three more energy sapping bridges he announced we had arrived at *Via Garibaldi*. It was to be another fifteen minutes before we had secured accommodation for ourselves at a small *pensione* which lay beyond a small fruit market. The rates were most favourable and the suite of rooms we took were the best they had to offer. They were certainly cramped quarters, but Holmes assured me they were fairly standard for hotels and lodgings in the city unless we desired luxury in the very finest hotels, usually located in the oldest and most beautiful *palazzos*. The manager was a *Signor* Grimaldi, who taking pity on his foot-sore guests, instructed his wife to prepare a local delicacy for us. The dish she favoured us with was *fegato alla veneziana,* a meal of liver with potato and polenta. By the time we had finished our repast the hour was quite late so we retired to our suite.

13

'Have you any idea as to where you would like to visit in Venice?' Holmes asked.

'I am content to be guided by you although having said that, I am quite keen to explore the basilica and the Doges' palace.'

'Two excellent choices, Watson. Shall we allot ourselves four days in the city?'

'If you think it ample, by all means.'

'It should be sufficient certainly and besides I know you are eager to rendezvous with the good Mrs Watson in Lyme Regis. How is she? Well and truly recovered from the ordeal she suffered at the hands of Stapleton?'

'She is a strong, resilient woman, Holmes. That is not to say there won't be scars, but she does not dwell upon the episode nor indeed speak of it.'

'She always struck me as a most dependable woman, calm, but with the ability to act swiftly and decisively in a crisis. She complements you perfectly, my dear fellow. What did you make of Pope Leo?'

'He is a most devout man, upright and single-minded. I fear he has not long left on this earth, I am actually surprised he has the energy he displayed to us for death certainly has him in its sights.'

'One supposes, Watson that his faith keeps him going. He still feels he still has work to do.'

'Faith is a great motivational force. It can truly work wonders even in our modern age. Perhaps mankind needs some form of faith more than ever before in a world where war becomes ever more commonplace.'

'To some extent you are right. Men of faith are natural leaders in times of crisis. They are looked up to and admired. It is a double-edged sword of course for throughout history men of faith have been a force for evil. One man's twisted ideology can create a movement that can wreak havoc in the name of faith or a sometimes unspecified god. Such men usually have no trouble in persuading others to follow them on their crusades for they are usually possessed of an unusual amount of charisma which makes it difficult to oppose their will. You are not a regular church-goer, Watson, but do you own up these days to having a faith or belief in a god?'

'As a child I was compelled to attend church regularly, but as I grew older my parents gave me a certain amount of latitude and free choice in the matter. Church attendance at that time ceased altogether apart from odd occasions in my life when I felt a need of spiritual comfort. Belief? Faith? I believe in a higher force, but do not seek to give it a name. What are your own feelings?'

'We have spoken of it before of course, but in general I put my faith in science. Faith may move mountains, but it is science we would look to for an explanation. So much of what we know about the world, science has shown us. The mystery of life is no longer a mystery.'

'Yet you would not attempt to argue that science has provided us with all the answers. There are still mysteries surrounding us, perhaps even some we will never find a solution to.'

'I agree wholeheartedly with you, Watson. Some things will forever be beyond our ken, maybe it is better that way; man arose from our environment and can never be expected to dominate it fully or be its master. As to my belief system I can honestly say I am unsure as to a creator or designer. The logician in me says it makes little sense to believe in a superhuman, all-powerful deity particularly when we look at the misery in the world. Would not a loving god try and rectify the conditions we live under?'

'The accepted principle in operation tells of the free choice mankind has been given to decide for itself how life should be lived. Until such time as there may be a reckoning.'

'The principle, then, appears to be one of 'give a man enough rope and he will hang himself' not particularly loving you would agree. All the same, I would not deny others their beliefs and faith. One has to plough one's own furrow in life.'

'I would imagine conversations like this to have taken place over the centuries. Whatever else we may think about religion, it has certainly been a driving force.'

'Indeed, Watson, but let's not forget how divisive organised religion has been and forever will be. It's just another form of the tribalism of ancient civilisations writ large. If we accept the premise of man being a natural aggressor while also accepting the notion of a creator then surely there is only one direction in which to apportion blame.'

'You are forgetting free will, Holmes.'

15

'Nay, Watson. I stated that man is a natural aggressor and I firmly believe that no one can in all honestly gainsay that. You see the distinction?'

'Yes. Perhaps this is one of the mysteries that will never be solved, the greatest of them all; where did we come from? Where do we go?'

'You are correct for everything follows from that and those two questions will remain as being fundamental to our lives. Venice will answer different questions for us; on art, on beauty and the ability of man to create a famed city in this watery wilderness. It is a city like no other on earth.'

'It seems barely conceivable that the city continues to stand when every sense tells you it should sink into the lagoon.'

'There is every evidence that the city is doing precisely that and the ways and means of preventing it will occupy the finest minds for many years to come, but with absolutely no guarantee of success. Nature, as she often does, may triumph in the end.'

'It's hard to imagine that all this may be lost one day.'

'It has often been the fate of great cities, to crumble into the dust. Not just cities, but whole civilisations have been lost.'

'*Tempus fugit*, Holmes.'

'Quite so, Watson. Well, I think I will turn in. Goodnight.'

I sat up a while longer, smoking a last pipe whilst contemplating and looking forward to my first full day in Venice.

The reality was somewhat different than I imagined.

'Leave them hanging. Cool, I like that. Not too sure about all that faith gubbins, bit boring maybe?'

'They have to discuss things, their characters demand it. Or they just say goodnight of course, but then the readers may think I lack imagination.'

'I think that ship has already sailed, mate. And you still slipped Beatrice and Lyme Regis in.'

'So? It's my story. I tell it how I want.'

'I've noticed. Do you really think this vast, imagined reading of public of yours want to know what Holmes and Watson ate?'

'It's called local colour.'

'And still not a sign of a countess let alone her gondolier alpha male.'

'Patience.'

Chapter Three

I had never realised what a noisy business it was to set up a fruit and vegetable stall until I was awoken by just that at six o' clock the following morning. It is my lot in life that once I am disturbed and brought out of my slumber then sleep will evade me.

Consequently I dressed and slipped out of the *pensione* to be greeted with a chorus of '*buongiornos*' from those whose racket had woken me. I nodded curtly, hoping this would suffice to show my displeasure. I took a few steps and turned back, thinking my behaviour rather churlish.

'*Buongiorno*,' I called, with as broad a smile as my disordered state would allow. I hoped my pronunciation was correct, it seemed to me to be a close approximation of their own greeting to me.

They smiled at me for a few seconds before settling back to the task at hand. The stall was fast becoming a riot of colour; yellows, greens and reds predominant. Already, there were would-be purchasers approaching, local matriarchs and younger wives who before and after making their purchases gathered together to converse animatedly. One or two looked in my direction and waved. I waved back, but feeling like an intruder, I turned and walked towards the lagoon.

There were a few people hurrying hither and thither as the city came to life, most content to offer the most cursory of nods as a sop to the etiquette of the morning. The air still had a damp quality to it, but the fog which had shrouded the city was gone. I made my way to St Mark's square, so empty and devoid of life now compared with how it was the previous day. I had heard the square described as 'The finest drawing-room in Europe' and nothing I saw disabused me of that notion. It was perhaps the best time to visit the square, in the eerie half-light of an early morning when all the buildings could be seen to their greatest advantage.

A few devout souls were entering the basilica for what I imagined was morning mass. I hesitated to join them, fearing myself an intruder once more, but my curiosity won the battle. I seated myself at the back and endeavoured to be as inconspicuous as was possible. The dim light of candles contributed to a feeling of sanctity as did the aroma of incense that pervaded my senses, leaving me with a calmness and serenity that I have rarely experienced.

Unsure as to what time *Signora* Grimaldi might be serving breakfast and even more unsure as to what that breakfast may consist of, I hastened back to the *pensione*. Holmes was leaning against the front of the establishment smoking a cigarette.

'Ah, Watson. I was about to organise a search party. Venice is probably the easiest city in the world in which to get lost. You probably noticed how I lost my bearings once or twice yesterday.'

'I can't say that I did, Holmes.'

'Well, they were only small errors and perhaps understandable in the conditions. I believe breakfast may be ready.''

'What may we expect?'

'A Venetian breakfast differs very little from a Roman one; we may expect ham, eggs, melon with lemon tea to wash it down.'

Although we certainly expected such a breakfast, none was to materialise for it seemed *Signora* Grimaldi had refused to come down to the kitchen and her husband had decided the making of breakfast for his guests could not possibly be construed as man's work. He moped around in the entrance hall bemoaning his fate. Holmes, whose Italian was workmanlike without ever approaching fluency, attempted to eke out what the problem was. Words passed back and forth with much gesticulating from Grimaldi. With a reassuring pat on Grimaldi's shoulder, Holmes turned to me.

'We must allow *Signora* Grimaldi some leeway for her brother has gone missing although her husband does not share her concern, adjudging the brother, Angelo, to be feckless and thinks him to be in a woman's company. He is what could be described as a ladies' man and when he forms new liaisons then his normal day to day life is of no consequence to him.'

'How long has he been missing?'

'Three days I am told and Maria, Grimaldi's wife now fears the worst. It is difficult enough for a gondolier to make a living this time of year without harming his income by disappearing for days.'

'Whatever he is doing or whoever he is spending his time with is no real concern of ours, Holmes.'

'Only in as much as it affects your digestive system, Watson. All the same, it wouldn't hurt to speak to Grimaldi's wife. I can at least offer her my assistance.'

'But we are in a city that I know not at all and you only a little. Your command of the Italian language although praiseworthy is, I'm sure you will agree, rather limited too. Further, there is no indication that this Angelo is missing in any real sense, that is to say that he may have decided on a whim to have a few days to himself or to spend a little time with a lady friend as Grimaldi suggests.'

'It would be the work of a few moments to visit the man's lodgings for instance and who knows, there may be a trail we can follow.'

'There may not be a trail. As you are fond of saying, we have no data to form an opinion.'

'If we find no trail or anything which is suggestive of foul play then I promise to devote my time to sharing and educating you in the sights of Venice. What do you say, Watson?'

Often I had found my will somewhat subservient to Holmes's resolve and once more I agreed to his arrangement whilst still harbouring and indeed voicing my doubts.

'Very well, but with the proviso that if you unearth any evidence or suspicion of criminal activity then you will go straight to the local police. Notwithstanding your own special skills, they are best equipped to carry out any investigation that may be required.'

'As you wish. I will ask *Signor* Grimaldi for permission to approach his wife.'

'Excellent. I will ask Grimaldi for permission to explore his kitchen!'

Holmes returned some twenty minutes later. Grimaldi had exhibited some degree of discomfiture during this time, evidently unused to having a strange Englishman visiting his wife in her room. This discomfiture had taken the form of muttering under his breath and raising his eyes towards the ceiling.

'I have the information I require, Watson. I can answer your questions along the way, should you have any.'

'My first question is this; would you care to go and sit down? Breakfast is nearly ready.'

'I do not feel the need of sustenance.'

'There are five other guests patiently waiting who have a contrary view and I am one of those five.'

'Mrs Hudson would be proud of your housekeeping skills, no less so, Mrs Watson. If you have supplemented your breakfast preparation talents with those of coffee-making then I can be persuaded to take part.'

Over breakfast Holmes gave me the gist of the information he had gleaned from Maria Grimaldi. This had been extracted in between her urgent entreaties to 'do something'.

What Holmes had learned was the following. 'Angelo is thirty-two years old and had been a gondolier for twelve years, a profession his father followed before a wrist injury forced him into alternative employment, that of a porter at a small glass-making company on the island of Murano. From all accounts he is well-liked and respected plus being exceedingly popular with the tourists for his knowledge of the city is second to none. Apparently he is particularly well acquainted with where to find both major and minor works of art, in which *scuola*, church or gallery. If he has a weakness, it's in his whole-hearted and enthusiastic appreciation of the fair sex although one doubts he has acquired your experience over three continents.'

'Have these dalliances resulted in Angelo disappearing on previous occasions?'

'They have.'

'Why should this occasion be treated any differently then?'

'The deciding factor is *Signora* Grimaldi's intuition. I am a great believer in the intuition of women, Watson.'

'Indeed, but that doesn't mean that she is correct in her assumptions.'

'I agree, but it will do no harm to look into the matter and try to alleviate her distress. Once we have done that we can indulge ourselves in sight-seeing to our heart's content. I take it you are now ready to go?'

'Once I have attended to the washing-up, yes.'

'Upon my word, Watson, you are taking your kitchen duties very seriously indeed. Perhaps you should stay on in Venice and open your own *pensione* or establish an Italian restaurant in Lyme Regis.'

'Very droll, Holmes. Why don't you indulge yourself with a pipe while I assist Grimaldi? I shall be a matter of minutes only.'

I was as good as my word and joined Holmes outside within fifteen minutes where he, despite my brevity, was pacing up and down, betraying his impatience with every footstep.

'Where are we bound, Holmes?'

'Angelo has a small apartment in *Cannaregio*.'

'Which is in Venice presumably?'

'Quite so. It is the northernmost *sestieri*, roughly speaking it runs from the station to the Rialto Bridge. Angelo's apartment lies just off the *Campo dei Mori*. He lives modestly although not without some luxury. Maria Grimaldi speaks of her brother as always having money which may tell us something of his character do you think?'

'I am not sure what you are implying.'

'It's just a possibility that I am considering. An Italian male in his thirties, handsome by all accounts, a gondolier who is in the company of tourists constantly, a known ladies' man who has money to spend.'

'Are you suggesting he is some kind of kept man? Receiving monies in return for his...er...company?'

'I am suggesting precisely that.'

'If that were so why would he be described as living modestly?'

'Most likely because his time would be spent away from his own apartment. The ladies he would seek to impress are more likely to want to entertain him on their own territory.'

'If your supposition is correct, and I have to say I am not in any way convinced of it due to the paucity of information we possess regarding Angelo, then his disappearance is explained. He has been spending these past three days earning an income of sorts far removed from that of a gondolier.'

During this conversation Holmes had been leading me through yet another maze of alleys with scarcely a pause in his stride. I consoled myself with the thought that soon I would have ample time to become acquainted with the intricacies of the city. By this time we had reached the Rialto Bridge. I paused halfway across to take in the wonderful view of the Grand Canal, but Holmes had marched on without me realising it and he was almost lost to my sight.

'No dawdling again please, Watson,' Holmes called.

With a grimace, I set off in pursuit. There were to be a few more twists and turns on our route before we entered the *Campo dei Mori.* Pinpointing Angelo's address, even though we turned out to be virtually on top of it, proved to be very tricky indeed, but eventually we climbed a set of stairs that took us to his apartment. The hollow sound that greeted Holmes's knock on the door told us of an empty apartment.

'Evidently Angelo is not home. I don't see what more we can do.'

'I hardly expected that he would be home, but now we are here we can best be employed by interviewing his neighbours. Any information they can supply however trivial it may seem could aid us.'

Four of the other five apartments were apparently empty for no one answered our earnest knocking. The door of the solitary apartment on the ground floor was opened an inch or two and all we could see of the occupant was a left eye which was protected by the bushiest of eyebrows and a left cheek adorned with flamboyant whiskers. The voice was muffled owing to the heavy door jammed in front of its owner's mouth.

'Good morning, gentlemen. Is there something I can help you with?'

Our surprise at being greeted in English became greater when the door swung fully open to reveal man who belonged to an earlier age. His style of dress was as dated as were his whiskers, which appeared to have a life of their own, being too large and bushy for the thin face they framed. I was forcibly reminded of a professor of English who taught me at Winchester, following his fall from grace at one of our smaller universities.

'You must forgive our intrusion,' said Holmes as we were invited in by an elaborate sweep of the arm. 'My name is Sherlock Holmes and this is my friend and colleague, Doctor Watson. We wish to ask you a few questions regarding Angelo who rents an apartment on the top floor here.'

'I see. Well, do come in. You are most cordially welcomed into my humble abode.'

This humble abode had the appearance of an ancient library, dust covered books filled every available space. Piles rose vertically defying gravity by refusing to topple. The large book cases pressed back against the walls were not just adorned with volumes of every size, but cobwebs hung down from the uppermost corners of each one. This chaos was negated slightly by the order I could see on a large desk situated under the window where pens paper and dictionaries were sitting quite neatly and most surprisingly, dust free.

'Please sit down,' he offered, then looked around, surprised by the fact there was precious little to sit on. He swept a few periodicals and journals onto the floor from the chairs they had been occupying and took his place on a well-upholstered chair behind the desk, evidently his usual habitat.

'Now we have a degree of comfort, we can proceed. Your names are known to me. Indeed, I have some of your work here, Doctor Watson. Tell me, do you realise how often you confuse your tenses? I would also recommend working on your subjunctives, they can be a little clumsy. Aside from those small criticisms, to which I might add your very singular approach to punctuation, I have enjoyed your accounts very much.'

'Bravo, Watson. You have an admirer who is not so blinded by your prose to spare you constructive criticism. Professor Collins, how came you to pitch up in Venice?'

'You know me then?'

'I can assure you I know nothing whatsoever about you other than the obvious facts that you graduated from Cambridge University, you suffered a painful divorce late in life, you have a son you love dearly, but are estranged from, you are a teacher of English at ridiculously low rates and you have lost your faith although that may be temporary.'

The recipient of these insights, smiled at Holmes and looked around the room.

'I have it, Mr Holmes. The diploma on the wall gave you both my name and university. The painful divorce...' He looked at his left hand. 'The mark of my wedding band is still obvious, hence it has been removed fairly recently. If it were anything other than a painful divorce, for instance a bereavement, than you might reasonably expect to me to wear it still. The photographs on the wall feature my son, the familial likeness is clear. There are no photographs of us together of a recent nature, so yes the deduction of an estrangement is sound enough. Now, the loss of faith? Let me see now. No, I confess I cannot see how you came by it.'

'The explanation is simple, Professor. There is a neck-chain with a cross on it in the corner of the room. Evidently thrown there by you. It is a chain that you were previously accustomed to wearing, even at this distance I can see grey hairs from your neck caught in the chain. I deduce your loss of faith to be temporary from the fact that the chain is still here and not been consigned to oblivion, although I admit I am on somewhat shaky ground there.'

'And the teaching at low rates?'

'That fact you teach is plain to see by the paraphernalia on your desk. You hardly live in the lap of luxury if I may be so bold, my dear sir, hence my deduction of low rates. Perhaps you see it as a vocation more than a living.'

'I do, Mr Holmes. I feel privileged to impart my knowledge to others. All I ask for is enough to cover my humble needs. I gravitated to Venice after my wife left me some five years ago. I intended to stay here just for a short while, but as there was nothing left for me in England, my son already being estranged from me, I elected to stay.'

'Are you familiar with Angelo, Professor?'

'I am. I have tutored him a little, in his chosen profession a few words of a foreign language can reap dividends when it comes to gratuities.'

'Is it just the English language your tutor your pupils in?' I asked.

'I have a smattering of knowledge of other tongues, certainly enough to help with common phrases, but English is my main language, followed by French, Spanish, German and Russian. Angelo learned a little of those languages, but his main goal was to become fluent in English. He is a very good student, attentive and punctually completes any work I give him. With the other languages I mention he was keen to learn not only the usual greetings and basic everyday polite exchanges, but also phrases more concerned with, how shall I put it gentlemen, the language of love.'

'We have heard him described as a ladies' man,' I interjected.

'A more than fitting description, Doctor Watson. He loves their company, they love his. It's an arrangement that entirely suits him and there is some financial gain, always a bonus for an often impoverished gondolier. You appear shocked, Doctor.'

'I am not shocked, Professor, I have seen too much of life to be shaken by a matter like this. Rather, I am surprised that Angelo would let slip something like this.'

Professor Collins gave a wheezy chuckle which turned into a prolonged coughing fit. When he had regained his composure he continued.

'You must excuse me, Doctor, my solitary life affords me very few opportunities for laughter. The fact of the matter is that Angelo did not let it slip, he likes to boast of it; his conquests and their generosity towards him. You may reason that he should be ashamed of what he does, but I say live and let live. He provides a service much like he does as a gondolier. Good luck to the fellow. But, tell me, has our romantic gondolier strayed into criminal activities? I cannot imagine Sherlock Holmes making a social call on a humble gondolier.'

'As far as we are aware he is an upright citizen notwithstanding his amorous adventures. We are here at his sister's request. She is worried because she has had no word from him for three days and her intuition leads her to believe there is something gravely wrong.'

'It is not unknown for Angelo to sequester himself away for a period of time with a new acquaintance, something his sister must be well aware of. Three days absence is by no means unusual for Angelo.'

'Do you know any of these acquaintances by name,' Holmes asked.

'Although Angelo is boastful, he does exercise a degree of discretion and has never revealed names to me. Of course I can deduce their nationalities by which language he needs to brush up on.'

'Has there been such a request recently?'

'There has indeed, Mr Holmes. Angelo was desirous of a little Russian to help smooth his way. Mostly phrases as I intimated before, redolent of the language of lovers.'

'When did he make this request?' Holmes asked.

'It was three weeks ago today, Mr Holmes. I especially remember the date for that morning I had decided to embark on a thorough cleaning of my apartment. But, as you can see, gentlemen, the spirit is willing, but the flesh rather less so.'

Holmes got to his feet, picked up a stack of periodicals from the floor and placed them back on the chair he had vacated.

'Thank you for your time, Professor Collins. You have been of great help.

'It was a great pleasure to meet you both and if I can be of any further assistance please feel free to call again.'

'Thank you. It's entirely possible that we will need to use a little Russian ourselves. If so, we will be in touch. *Arrivederci.*'

'Well, Holmes,' I said, as we entered the *campo* once more, 'there is nothing more we can do.'

'I think there are several courses of action open to us. There can't be that many Russians in Venice that one of their number cannot be tracked down. Angelo may have been the very soul of discretion with the professor, but he may be less inclined to be so with his fellow gondoliers; interviewing them may bear fruit.'

'We do not know who his closest colleagues are and we have no clues as to who this Russian is.'

'I think, Watson, that we can at least assign a gender to the Russian in question.'

'A Russian needle in an Italian haystack.'

'Oh, we can do better than that I am sure. Come, we will report back to Maria Grimaldi who can probably supply us with names of some of her brother's fellow gondoliers. Along the way, Watson, we will begin our sight-seeing. I have in mind a small church that you will find most interesting.'

'Is this where it turns into a travelogue?'

'I think the readers want a little bit of Venice in there. No good setting it there otherwise. Local colour again.'

'This professor chap, does he appear again?'

'No, why?'

'That's just it...why? Why is he there, mate?'

'Local colour.'

'If you want colour, put a rainbow in it! And...'

'Yes?'

'Still no gondolier or Russian countess!'

6987. P. Z. - VENEZIA. PALAZZO REZZONICO.

8691. P. Z. - VENEZIA PALAZZO DEI DOGI E PALAZZO REALE.

Chapter Four

As we exited the *campo* Holmes paused. 'What do you make of that, Watson?'

'That statue? It look a little odd to me, comical even.'

'I agree, but I was thinking of the stone box that has the appearance of a lion's mouth.'

'Is it an early form of post-box?'

'In a manner of speaking, yes. Venetians were very much encouraged by the state to effectively spy on their neighbours, friends and family. These stone boxes were a means of conveying residents' complaints which could be both trivial and serious. If your neighbour was excessively noisy or swore too much for your liking then he could be fined, but a report of treason or a conspiracy could ultimately lead to execution. In the latter days of the Republic such notes could lead to punishment without trial for the supposed offenders. Do you see the inscription on this example?'

I bent down and peered at it, it was not easy to decipher, but I read it as; *Bestemmiate no piu 'e date Gloria a Dio*. Something to the glory of God?'

'Well deduced although that part was hardly difficult. It translates as; *Swear no more and give glory to God.*'

We continued on our way and retraced our steps, at least until Holmes veered off to the right suddenly, then turned north. We traversed a wide canal and Holmes walked a few yards to his right.

'There you are, Watson. The church of *Madonna dell'orto*.'

What I saw in front of me was a church set back from the canal with a wide courtyard in front of it. The façade was ornate with a large circular window above the doorway that reminded me of one at York Minster.

'The real treasures are inside, Watson. Tintoretto is buried here and some of his finest works adorn the walls and chapels. I can recount to you an amusing tale concerning Tintoretto and this church.'

'I usually find your amusing tales are anything but, Holmes!'

'The fault must lie with your interpretation, my dear fellow. Tintoretto took refuge in the church from a furious client, in this case a doge for he had painted cuckold's horns to a portrait of the doge that had already been rejected by the sitter. The doge offered to forget and forgive the insult if Tintoretto agreed to decorate the church. The doge's idea was that this would keep Tintoretto busy for many years, but the artist had other ideas and completed his work here in six months.'

'Remarkable, Holmes.'

'Even more so when you look at his paintings of the *Last Judgment* and *The Making of the Golden Calf*. They are quite something are they not?'

'They are very striking indeed.'

'I have seldom seen better depictions of those two events. The other paintings within the church are of less interest, but still fine examples of their kind. The Last Judgment reigns supreme and I believe cannot be eclipsed. Tintoretto lived just a few yards away on the *Fondamenta dei Mori*. If you try not to tarry too long in here, Watson, I will show you the house before we leave for *Via Garibaldi*.'

I wandered around the church, all the time conscious of Holmes drumming his fingers on the back of one of the pews. I was determined not to respond in any way to Holmes's impatience, after all, it was his idea to come and visit this church and I did not see the necessity of making the visit a brief one. Once I had taken my fill of the sights, I motioned to Holmes that I was ready. True to his word, Holmes showed me the house where Tintoretto and lived and worked and indeed died in 1594. Pronouncing myself satisfied, we set off on the walk back to the Grimaldi's *pensione*.

We had scarcely walked one hundred yards when we heard excited shouting and cries. Holmes, unerringly, headed towards the source of these sounds. In a maze of alleyways we came to a small bridge and were met with the sad sight of a body being brought up out of the canal which flowed under it. Three men were hoisting it with the aid of a fourth man who was waist high in the water steadying it.

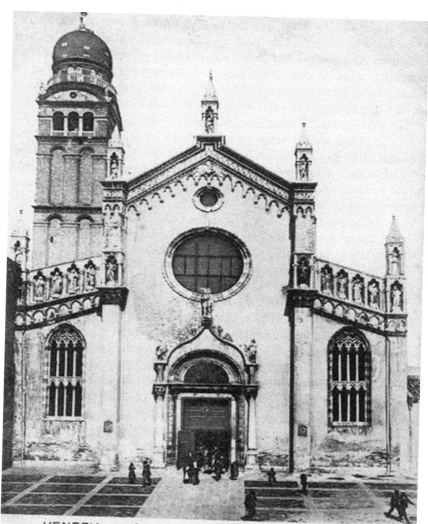

VENEZIA — Chiesa della Madonna dell' Orto (1473)

They worked steadily inch by inch until at last their cargo was brought ashore. The body was that of a youngish man who bore marks of violence upon him. The head injuries I could see certainly looked severe although without a closer examination it would impossible to determine what caused them; they may have resulted from a fall or equally have been inflicted deliberately. Holmes nudged me forward while whispering in my ear. I took my cue from him.

'*Io medico,*' I cried, pushing my way through.

I examined the corpse as quickly as I could, conscious of the fact that I had no jurisdiction here and when the authorities arrived the official wheels would be set in motion and my part in the proceedings would be made redundant. There were further injuries; broken ribs and a broken arm amongst them.

'It's murder, Holmes. There can be no doubt.'

There were murmurs of *e stato omicidio* and *un terribile omicidio* from the growing crowd of bystanders.

'How old would you say he was?'

'Early thirties at the most, Holmes. You don't think...'

'We have to admit the possibility.'

'Poor Maria,' I said, as I got to my feet.

The clattering of approaching feet signalled the arrival of the police, two uniformed officers of the *polizia locale*. They quickly took charge of the situation and cleared an area around the corpse. While one examined the body, the other asked questions of the onlookers that even with my limited Italian I recognised chiefly as Who? When? How? Someone pointed at me and said, *medico* and mimed my examination of the body. I knelt down once more and pointed out the injuries to the officers whilst demonstrating on my own body what I thought had transpired. Holmes scribbled something on a scrap of paper and handed it to one of the officers with a few simple words of explanation.

'The Garibaldis' address, Watson. It is a worthwhile starting point for their investigation.'

'If it is indeed Angelo.'

'I am convinced of it.'

'Then our part in this drama is over.'

'Not necessarily. I feel a responsibility here not least to Maria Grimaldi.'

'But she is not a client, Holmes, not in any real sense.'

'I have heard her entreaties, she is client enough for me. I think we should go and prepare the way for the bad news that is bearing down on her.'

'I do not wish to labour the point, but you did agree that should there be any indication of criminal activity then you would hand over the matter to the proper authorities.'

'True, but the local police are now on the scene regardless of my involving them. I maintain my right to look into this matter.'

'But, that's just it. You have no rights or official standing here. One hardly expects the Venice police welcoming a holiday-maker into their ranks no matter how illustrious a career he may have.'

'You have a point of course, but we have overcome such obstacles before.'

Holmes took out one of his cards and handed it to the nearest of the policemen who numbers had been swollen by the appearance of five more officers. Our route back to *Via Garibaldi* was subtly altered, uncharitably I thought this may have been due to Holmes getting lost, but even had this been the case he would have been unlikely to admit it. We found ourselves outside the main entrance to the *Arsenale*, the centre of Venice's shipbuilding and navy for centuries. I scarcely had time to appreciate the impressive gateway with its majestic plinths with massive carved lion's heads atop each one for Holmes was hurrying on.

'Mr Holmes!'

I looked around to see a tall man approaching us, arm outstretched.

Holmes had stopped, looking as startled as I was to hear his name being called.

'Well, well,' he said, One can scarcely move in Italy without tumbling over you, Peterson.'

'Hardly, Mr Holmes, it was eleven years ago after all, but given your penchant for exaggeration I can forgive the remark.'

'Thank you for your exoneration. Watson, may I introduce Stafford Peterson, a detective of sorts...'

'...of sorts?'

'Indeed. I made the acquaintance of Peterson in Florence eleven years ago when he persuaded me, against my better judgment I might add, to look into the theft of the Botticelli painting *Spring* from the Uffizi gallery.'

'I am pleased to meet you, Mr Peterson.'

'Thank you, Doctor Watson.'

'Be careful in your dealings with Peterson for he exhibits a pawky humour not unlike your own which he seeks to introduce at the most inappropriate times. We are on a urgent mission, Peterson, but if you wish, we can share a coffee together shortly. I am intrigued as to how you have been spending your time these past few years. There is a coffee shop at the southern end of *Via Garibaldi*, be good enough to join us there in fifteen minutes.'

As we walked on I asked Holmes about the Botticelli theft.

'I assume you recovered the painting, Holmes?'

'Indeed. It was a fairly simple matter involving a corrupt Italian policeman and a peer of the realm.'

'I do not recall reading about such a case in the newspapers and surely a peer involved in such a theft would have merited a few paragraphs in the broadsheets.'

'This particular peer, whom even now I am not at liberty to name, was persuaded to assist us in the taking of his fellow conspirators and certain promises were made on both sides which enabled him to keep his freedom. He knows that I have kept my eye on him since and consequently he is a changed man.'

'I am none too comfortable with knowing that such persons can, in effect, get away with their crimes.'

'Yet you yourself exonerated Captain Croker in the Abbey Grange affair.'

'The circumstances were different.'

'Yes, for Jack Croker killed a man as opposed to merely stealing a Renaissance painting.'

'An act of self-defence only. Presumably your peer did not steal the painting by accident!'

Further discussion on the subject was postponed for as we arrived at the *pensione* we found the police had beaten us to it and we were met with the sad sight of Maria Grimaldi, grief-stricken, being escorted out of the building. Holmes had a brief kindly word with her before her husband came out to join her.

'She has the sad task of identifying the body. Perhaps we had better delay asking any questions of her until tomorrow.'

'Only if she is up to it, she may remain in shock for several days to come.'

'I will only proceed on your say so, Watson. Now, we will join Peterson for that welcome coffee.'

The small coffee house was thriving if the number of occupied tables was anything to go by. The aroma of the freshly brewed coffee and the pastries on offer was quite a heady mix. The warmth therein was most welcome too for outside the temperature was dropping as the fog returned.

Peterson was already ensconced in the corner furthest from the bar and beckoned us over.

'I favour the *macchiato*, it is strong, but with a delicate taste,' he announced.

'Thank you for your recommendation. We may even act on it,' said Holmes as we sat down. The waiter appeared immediately. Holmes ordered for both of us, *'Due macchiatos per favore. Grazie.'*

'Your Italian has not noticeably improved in the intervening years, Mr Holmes.'

'Nor your wit, Peterson. Are you still making a living in the same manner?'

'Yes, but you could say I am rather more official these days. You are looking at a legitimate member of the police force here.'

'How did that come about?'

'It has its roots in that case in Florence. *Vice-Questore* Bonetti was rather pleased with my handling of the investigation and my exposing of Niccolo Adduci and decided that I was the best man to succeed him in the *offizio culturale*. Naturally, I concurred with him.'

'Naturally. I seem to recall the little matter of my own involvement.'

'I cannot deny that you were of some help to me.'

'Your generosity of spirit does you great credit, Peterson. I cannot ascribe the same credit to your memory, but please continue.'

'I functioned as head of that department until two years ago when I was offered a similar position here with a salary more commensurate with my skills.'

'You have done well for yourself. I trust the Florentine authorities were suitably harsh with Adduci.'

'Fifteen years' hard labour was their decision. William Redmayne was treated lightly by comparison, just ten years.'

I shifted my weight forward, reminding both men of my presence.

'If I may ask a question,' I ventured.

'Of course, Doctor.'

'I presume this Redmayne was another conspirator in the Botticelli theft. He is English I take it?'

'No, he is one of the fiery Sicilian Redmaynes.'

'I did warn you about Peterson's fleeting acquaintance with humour, Watson.'

'Very droll I am sure. You are attached to the police here then?'

'Rather more than attached. I am in charge of my own department here much as I was in Florence. We specialise in what you may term 'crimes against culture'. Art theft, icon theft, relic theft. Vandalism in galleries, churches and museums. We oversee sales and transportation of art treasures, ensuring all official channels are adhered to and all paperwork is correctly made out. We are a small department, but well organised.'

'And are you plagued by much in the way of art theft?' I asked.

'We deal mostly with small fry, but occasionally a gang from further afield will attempt to muscle in and make their presence felt. There is something of the kind happening right now as it happens.'

Holmes leaned forward, eyes shining, suddenly alert.

'Perhaps you could enlighten us, Peterson.'

'Do you know a woman who calls herself Countess Lenska? I say 'calls herself' because there is no reason to believe she has any right to a title. I believe her to be the same woman who has been known as Madam Orlov.'

'I am familiar with the name, the woman and her alleged deeds. She is in Venice?'

'My word, Mr Holmes, your deductive skills are still formidable!'

'Thank you, your mocking humour is not altogether unpleasing,' said Holmes, chuckling softly.

I will confess to feeling something akin to a pang of jealousy observing these two men who obviously enjoyed each other's company, engaging in this banter. As with all my unworthy thoughts, I quickly pushed it away and asked another question.

'I have never heard either name, could I be enlightened?'

'Of course, Doctor. Let's refer to her as Countess Lenska. She is a lady of means who has no scruples as to how she acquires those means. She and her entourage travel throughout Europe and wherever she pitches up trouble surely follows. It may be the theft of baubles, jewels or paintings, most of which are believed to be sold on to collectors to fund her lavish lifestyle. No crime, however, has ever been laid at her door. There is a web of silence amongst her entourage and clients which has proved impossible to break down and believe me there have been many attempts throughout the continent to infiltrate her circle, but all to no avail. In fact, four years ago she arrived in Florence and through contacts in the underbelly of Florentine life we heard whispers of an audacious attempt to steal treasures from the *duomo* itself.'

'Were you able to thwart her plans?'

'Yes, Doctor, but at a cost. Although much of her life is a mystery in spite of being a prominent figure in social circles wherever she goes, she is known to have, shall we say, a predilection for young men. We devised a plan whereby one of our young officers, a strikingly handsome man, would inveigle himself into her close circle, gain her trust and be handily placed to get wind of any planned theft. He reported to me personally, not at the *Questore* for he had been expressly forbidden from being seen in the vicinity, but instead we met under cover of darkness in coffee shops, bars and the like. At each of these meetings he reported that he was making good progress. Then, nothing.'

'Nothing?'

'Indeed, Doctor Watson. At first I thought he had defected as it were, but I decided he was far too conscientious an officer for that to happen. A few days later the Countess, with her acolytes left the city. One day after that, Officer Sandro Mazzini's body was found in disused railway sidings. He had been beaten almost beyond recognition and there were signs of torture upon the body. The hardest thing I have ever had to do is to relate the news of his death to his mother. Of course, you say all the right things; he was a brave man, he died the death of a hero, but the fact of it is, that he died a scared young man, alone and in unimaginable pain and I can never forget it was me that sent him to his death.'

Suddenly, Stafford Peterson the joker was gone and another pain-wracked Peterson took his place. Other customers swivelled their heads and looked on as Peterson openly wept, his head bent and his whole body convulsed in grief. Both Holmes and myself tried to calm with the usual platitudes that polite society dictates we employ, but our words of sympathy had little effect. Eventually the tears dried and he met our gaze.

'My apologies, gentlemen. Occasionally old wounds open up and my emotions are as fresh to me now as they were then. You see, the Countess is not a social butterfly flitting from ball to ball while engaging in some light-hearted pilfering, but she is highly dangerous, employing those who will stop at nothing to protect her. And now she is here.

'How long has she been here?'

'A little over four weeks and so far, all is quiet, at least in so far as we can attribute any crime to her. There has been the theft of a couple of pictures, both of the Annunciation by minor Venetian painters, from two churches, but nothing other than that.'

'I may be about to shatter your comparative silence,' said Holmes and he proceeded to tell Peterson all we learned about Angelo and his tragic death.

Peterson whistled. 'I am inclined to agree with you, I have been known to occasionally after all. Angelo must have seen something or heard something he was not supposed to. How do we proceed?'

'With more coffee inside us, shall I order?'

'I shall do it, Holmes. I need to practise my Italian.'

'I certainly agree with you there, my dear fellow!'

I took a deep breath and as a waiter passed by, I hailed him.

'Tre macchiatos per favore. Grazie.'

Holmes applauded. 'Excellent, Watson, you would surely be mistaken for an Italian were it not for your reticence, demeanour, clothes and your moustache.'

Once the coffees had arrived we set about tackling the problem of the so-called Russian Countess.

'Where has she based herself for her stay in Venice?' Holmes asked.

'She has taken the top two floors of the Hotel Vivaldi. As far as we can ascertain she has with her three young women and two particularly burly men who are more bodyguards than factotums. Whenever she leaves the hotel she has the company of at least two of those five. I must confess she is quite an arresting sight; her dresses have plunging necklines which would most likely result in her arrest in a less enlightened city. Her age is unknown, but underneath the copious face paint I suspect you would find a woman in her fifties.'

'I know I am probably being naive,' I said, 'but is it not possible to take her into custody while you search for incriminating evidence?'

'Would that I could, Doctor, but she moves in exalted circles with friends in very high places. I fear I would have a diplomatic incident on my hands which would not sit well with the city fathers. No, we need to work stealthily to achieve results in order to close the net around her. Vigilance is needed for just one slip from one of the gang could be their downfall.'

'I assume they are shadowed by your men wherever they go?'

'Yes, by my men and men that *Vice-Questore* Rossi can spare. Nothing untoward has been noted. Of course our shadowing only works up to a point for when they are safely ensconced in the Vivaldi they can make their plans safely.'

'Have you probed for weaknesses in the individual members of her entourage?' Holmes asked.

'I fear they cannot be bought. Their mistress is more than generous and they are given liberty to enjoy their own pleasures. It may be that she has a hold on them in other ways.'

'Blackmail?'

'Some kind of emotional leverage I suspect, Doctor, but it is supposition only.'

'The pleasures you say they enjoy, Peterson, does that present an opening, an opportunity that can be exploited?' Holmes asked.

'The men seem to have no pleasure other than gambling and one supposes, they way they are built, violence. The women, at any rate two of them if are observations are correct, share their mistresses' love for men although they seem to be drawn towards the older variety.'

'I, that is we, have an obligation towards Maria Grimaldi, but as our interests overlap we should work together towards a common end unless *Vice-Questore* Rossi should voice any objection.'

43

'He would fall in line with my wishes I am sure; he has a copy of one of Doctor Watson's volumes on his bookcase in his office and often refers to your exploits. He was particularly impressed with your assistance in the Adduci case and the way you took your lead from me.'

'Are you not a little dissatisfied with your low salary, Peterson?'

'My low salary?'

'Earlier you intimated that you were paid with a rate commensurate with your skills. I naturally thought that you must be in receipt of an extremely low salary.'

'Mr Holmes,' chuckled Peterson, 'for only the second time ever, you have made me laugh. Now, what say we take a stroll down to the Hotel Vivaldi? I cannot promise you much by way of spectacle, but it's possible we may have sight of our quarry.'

'An excellent idea.'

'Stafford Peterson might confuse folk, mate.'

'I don't see why.'

'He's not canon is he? People like to have things how they should be.'

'I can't just use characters from ACD, it would show a lack of imagination.'

'Yeah, well I've never been convinced by your imagination.'

'Charming.'

'No offence, mate.'

'Cheers.'

'I think I know where you are going with it.'

'Is it that obvious?'

'As always.'

'Charming.'

Chapter Five

The Hotel Vivaldi was was just a hundred yards or so along that most stately of waterfronts the *Riva degli Schiavoni*. It was named for the Dalmatian merchants who used to tie up their boats, vessels laden with wares from the East. The quayside was still a bustling hive of activity with traders competing to sell knick-knacks to the tourists who wandered the length of the quay.

Peterson approached one of these traders who was selling rather cheap looking models of gondolas. They spoke to each other for a few moments before Peterson rejoined us.

'One of my men as I am sure you deduced. None of the travelling party as have yet surfaced. The men were at the casino until the early hours. Two of the women ventured out yesterday evening, returning to the hotel with a man, who they appeared to be good-naturedly fighting over although one suspects they, how shall I put it, shared him.'

'I am surprised a respectable hotel would allow guests to bring people back to the hotel in that manner.'

'Money talks, Doctor and if guests who are willing to spend a small fortune on suites of rooms are sufficiently discreet in their liaisons then the hotel management will gladly turn a blind eye.'

'Does someone watch the hotel at night?' Holmes asked.

'We do not employ anyone to watch from the outside at night, their presence could easily be detected, but we have a man on the inside who is to all intents and purposes a member of the hotel cleaning staff. He is under strict instructions to watch only not to interfere with the Countess's party in any way.'

'Are all the members of the entourage Russian?' I asked.

'As to that, we cannot be certain that Lenska herself is Russian. She speaks English with a thick accent which could be Middle European or just an affectation. Her Italian is limited apparently. The three young women with her speak in French to each other although it is thought that one of the girls, who calls herself Emmeline could be English. We believe the other two are Marguerite and Anna. They appear to be in their twenties. We have no names for the men for they never address each other by name. We have been awaiting intelligence from certain European police forces, including Scotland Yard, which may give us more information.'

The three of us looked more than a little conspicuous outside the hotel so I excused myself and decided to explore a church a few yards away. A board outside declared it to be the *Chiesa La Pieta*. It was a handsome looking building with an interior to match, in particular there was a very fine ceiling painting; a small leaflet I picked up informed that the artist was Giambattista Tiepolo. I did not know the name, but if there were more examples of his work in Venice then I was determined to seek them out. *La Pieta* it transpired was known as Vivaldi's church after Antonio Vivaldi, the composer who was concert-master here from 1705 to 1740. I spent a full thirty minutes in the church in silent contemplation away from the criminal elements that even this most beautiful of cities had in its midst, reasoning that if I was needed then Holmes would seek me out.

When I exited the church I found that for the first time the sun was trying to make its presence felt. The dark clouds and the drizzle which seemed to be a permanent feature of the day were battling hard to retain their supremacy, but it looked as though the sun would be the victor.

Holmes and Peterson were conversing by a gondola stand when a low whistle by Peterson's man caused us all to look in the direction of the hotel. Coming out was a party of five people; three women and two men. The woman at the centre of this group was small in stature yet obviously dominant. Her make-up was heavily applied, but even so did not obscure a natural beauty. She was positively festooned in jewellery, with rings on each and every finger and a colourful, gaudy chain around her neck. Her dress, while within the bounds of common decency, was designed to concentrate attention on her ample bosom. The younger women who flanked her took their cue in dress from her, but judging by the slight restraint they showed I reckoned it would be a cardinal sin on their part to outdo their mistress in any way.

The men were both powerfully built looking every inch the bruisers they probably were. The last place you would wish to encounter these men would be a dark alley in Venice.

I stayed outside the church while this strange caravan passed by. One of the young women, whose blonde hair hung loosely below her bonnet, caught my eye and smiled at me. Without thinking, I returned her smile and she giggled coquettishly and pointed me out to her companions.

'Yet another conquest I see, Watson,' said Holmes as he and Peterson came over to join me. 'Which of the girls has fallen for Watson, Peterson?

'I believe it was Emmeline.'

The irony of the situation was not lost on me. I had not joined Holmes and Peterson for fear of bringing attention to ourselves, yet I had accomplished that feat alone. Just ahead of us on a bridge where tourists strained for the best view of the Bridge of Sighs, one of the most famous of Venice's landmarks, a man who was standing engrossed in a newspaper folded the paper under his arm and fell into step behind the Countess and her companions. I thought this most obvious and said as much to Peterson.

'You are right of course, Doctor and were he one of our men I would reprimand him, but I have no idea who he is. Our man, is ahead of the group, ostensibly sweeping the path. Well, he is sweeping the path actually and making a very good fist of it too, perhaps I should suggest he pursues it as an alternative career.'

As I watched, he carried on with his sweeping duties as the group passed him, then after allowing them to forge on ahead, he picked up his broom and large dustpan and followed them discreetly.

'Where do they go on these perambulations of theirs?' Holmes asked.

'There is no fixed route they adhere to. *Scuolas*, churches, galleries, all the usual sights. Sometimes it is just a walk and nothing else.'

'Far be it from me to impugn your team of shadowers, but the Countess would have met and entertained Angelo on more than a few occasions. Was that logged or noted? How many men do you employ in this manner? If the entourage splits into, say, three groups, who do you elect to follow? Or have you the manpower to cover all eventualities? You see, in spite of this ongoing observation at least one of their number murdered and then dumped Angelo's body, avoiding detection whilst doing so.'

'I would be the first to admit that this is far from a perfect operation. We are not equipped to deal with such surveillance and *Vice-Questore* Rossi is hampered by a wholly inadequate budget. We do the best we can with the resources we have at our disposal.'

'My dear Peterson, it was not a criticism.'

'Oddly enough, it sounded very much like it.'

'I have an idea,' I ventured, 'can not one of these men of Lenska's be tempted into an indiscretion, such as a street fight, enabling the police to arrest him?'

'I would imagine it could be accomplished very easily yet it would not advance our cause at all. The most likely result would be a fine which would be duly paid by the Countess. Even the threat of a gaol term would be unlikely to loosen tongues I am sad to say, Doctor.'

'There must be something we can do!' I protested.

At that precise moment an idea formed in my head, a wild outlandish idea, but one that I thought may pay dividends. If I embarked on this course of action I would, certainly initially, have to act alone. My thoughts flew to Beatrice so many miles away; could I even contemplate an action such as this without consulting her? Would she expressly forbid it? All I knew was that we had to do something and to my mind I was the ideal man to act. The other dilemma I had was just how could I put my plan into operation without the knowledge of Holmes? If we had been in London I could have excused myself with the explanation of an urgent telegram to be sent and take myself off to Wigmore Street post office. Venice was another matter. My dilemma was solved by Holmes himself

'Are you all right, Watson? You appear to be lost in thought. Is your mind straying to Lyme Regis?'

'In a manner of speaking, Holmes, but mostly I feel a little weary.'

'We are going to pay a visit to *Vice-Questore* Rossi. Would you rather have a little time to yourself? We can meet up later and share our news, should we have any, with you.'

'I think I will go and seat myself in the *piazza* and watch the world go by.'

'If you go any further afield do try not to get lost, Watson. Goodbye for now.'

I was not happy deceiving Holmes, but I knew if I apprised him of my plan he would be sure to talk me out of it This was a time I had to be strong no matter how hard the road ahead may prove to be.

There was no sign of my quarry in the *Piazza San Marco* and there was no way of determining the direction they had taken. With no firm plan in mind, I headed in a vague northerly direction until I came to the Rialto Bridge. I kept going north past the markets, all the time questioning my sanity. Eventually I found myself in a large square. A plaque on a nearby wall informed me I was now in the *Campo San Polo*.

There were a few tourists milling around enjoying the afternoon sun which gave a special radiance to the buildings in the square. I ambled through the square and came into another *campo*. As I admired from a distance a particularly striking, large church I saw the Countess and her entourage enter the square from a narrow alleyway. The two men separated from the group and headed east and the women, linking hands entered the church.

My resolve held and allowing them five minutes, I walked over and entered the church also which proclaimed itself to be the *Santa Maria Gloriosa Dei Frari*. They were admiring the monuments and paintings on the left and wishing the encounter to be as accidental as I could possibly make it, I elected to wander down the right hand side keeping pace with them, but not once looking in their direction.

Passing a fine wooden statue of St John the Baptist I found myself by the high altar. I heard giggling nearby and as I turned round I was face to face with the young woman Peterson had identified as Emmeline. She smiled at me as she had before and pointed upwards. I followed her gaze.

'Assumption,' she said, smiling still. 'Titian.'

'Ah, wonderful,' I enthused.

'*Oui, monsieur, magnifique.*'

Perhaps Peterson had been mistaken and Emmeline was not English after all, but I elected to answer in English regardless.

'I quite agree, it is an awe-inspiring sight.'

The other young woman reached out and grasped my arm.

'*Non, Marguerite. Il est mien.*'

'*Il est trop vieux, meme pour vous!*'

I honestly thought they were going to come to blows, but they seemed satisfied with a little pushing and shoving. The Countess looked on with a look of amusement on her face before stepping in.

'*Halte. Voici un maison de Dieu.*'

They scowled at each other, but put an end to their argument which I suspected was nothing more than play-acting for my benefit.

Countess Lenska looked me in the eye, an action which unnerved me for she reminded me of nothing less than a cobra, poised to strike.

'*Mi dispiace,*' she said.

I shrugged my shoulders, doing my very best to portray a simple Englishman abroad.

'*Inglese.*'

'I zee. Zen I must offer my apologies for the badness of my girls.'

'Think nothing of it. I am sure they are most charming young women,' I replied, smiling at Emmeline.

'Zis is most understanding of you. *Venir avec quelqu'un.*'

Emmeline and Marguerite returned to the Countess's side. Emmeline exchanged a few words in French with her mistress and then addressed me.

'My friends are a little busy for a while. Would you take pity on a poor unchaperoned girl and allow her some time in your company?'

'My dear young lady, it would be a great honour for me. I am John Williams.'

'Emmeline Cousins.'

We explored the rest of the church together, expressing our mutual admiration of the art on view. From the *Frari* we made our way to the church of *San Polo*. Emmeline pointed out the very fine portal before we entered. Inside there was a striking, brooding *Last Supper* by

Tintoretto which Emmeline enthused over although Tiepolo's *Via Crucis* was much more to my liking.

Emmeline was so charming and sweet that I had to keep reminding myself that she was possibly part of a criminal enterprise and a lady of loose morals too from all accounts. Opposite the church stood a rose-coloured *palazzo* in which, she informed me that Casanova had once resided when young.

'Casanova was the great seducer whose antics outraged Venetian society. Are you like Casanova at all, John?'

'I am not sure I have ever seen a likeness of him, but I doubt it.'

'Oh, John, you are teasing. You know what I meant.'

Emmeline's direct ways left me feeling most uncomfortable. I had not known a young woman to be this forward. I knew I was acting with the noblest of motives and in spite of my discomfort I had no recourse, but to continue my course of action.

'I hardly think I fall into that category, Emmeline.'

'You need someone to bring out that side of you,' she giggled.

'I fear I am too old and set in my ways to change now,' I responded. 'No one would wish to bring out that side of me for one thing.'

'I would, John...and could.'

'Well, we could discuss it over lunch if you wish.'

'That would be lovely. I know a little *ristorante*, it is a little expensive, but I can just tell you are a generous man.'

The *ristorante* she had in mind was ten minutes walk away in the *sestieri* of *Dorsoduro*. It occupied a fine position, overlooking the grand canal, next door to the church of *Santa Maria della Salute*. To say the ristorante was a little expensive was akin to saying Pope Leo was slightly religious. Emmeline was certainly possessed of an extremely healthy appetite, I wondered how her slender frame could co-exist peaceably with her food intake. We talked while we ate.

'Are you married, John?'

'No, I have never been fortunate in that regard,' I said, silently mouthing my apologies to Beatrice.

'Yet you wear a wedding band...'

'I, well, that is to say I...'

'Oh, John. If you are married, just admit it. I have no objection to the company of someone else's husband.'

'I am married, yes.'

'But here alone?'

'With friends, but they had their own agenda today.'

'How lucky that you fell into my lap. And I have to tell you, John, that I am happy to have you in my lap.'

I fear I blushed at that point, causing her no little amusement and certainly did nothing to moderate her amorous attentions which became more explicit as the wine took hold. I asked about her life and how she came to be in Venice.

This is what she told me: She was born in Guildford and her star burned brightly at school, but a certain incident, that she didn't enlarge on other than to say she was an innocent victim, resulted in her expulsion. She then took up a position in an art gallery which resulted not only in an appreciation of art, but also marriage to the gallery owner. When he died, leaving her his fortune, she elected to travel being young enough and having money enough to live life to the full. In between various love affairs, the details of which I will gloss over, she exhausted most of her new-found wealth and was fortunate enough to meet Countess Lenska in Budapest. She became a general help, not a servant she stressed to me, and has stayed with her these past six years. Marguerite and Anna threw in their lot with the Countess in Paris four years ago.

'When I saw you earlier today I could not help, but notice two very powerful looking men with you.'

'Ah, John, you are jealous. Don't worry, they are not my lovers although there was one time when...but perhaps you do not wish to hear such things.'

I shook my head vigorously.

'Madam employs them, they are useful to her.'

'Not as....'

'No,' she laughed, 'she prefers the company of younger men and women. I am sure you know what I mean, John.'

I did, but I certainly did not feel the need to elaborate on it.

'What does Countess Lenska do? How does she come by her money?'

Emmeline replied, smiling sweetly, but with steel in her voice, 'Why do you want to know? I thought it was me you were interested in...wouldn't you like to know more about me? I would gladly open up to you, John.'

'Yes, you are quite right, you are more than fascinating enough for me.'

'That pleases me. You can please me more by ordering me some *tiramisu*.'

Her appetite for dessert was undiminished by the two courses she had already eaten. My worry was just how much the bill would come to. There was certainly no suggestion that the cost would be shared and truth be told, I could hardly suggest it for my plan would surely fall at the first hurdle if I did so. The attraction older men held for the three girls had just as much to do with their wallets as their courtship.

'Tell me what you do, John. How do you earn your money?'

I had anticipated the question, but had not as yet come up with a fully-fledged answer. I thought it best to come as close to the truth as I could in case awkward questions were asked later.

'I am a surgeon. Partly retired now.'

'That sounds very exciting.'

'Hardly, it involves long hours, steady nerves and an extraordinary dedication. I rose to the top of my profession and became quite celebrated for pioneering some quite new procedures, some of which I used when operating on some of the most noble men and women in Britain.'

'You had power then?'

'A certain amount of it yes, Emmeline.'

'I do like powerful men, John. Would you like to walk me back to the hotel, it's the Hotel Vivaldi.'

'Yes, I know.'

'What? How do you know?'

'I...well...I don't actually know,' I blustered, 'but when I saw you this morning by the hotel I naturally assumed you had come out of its doors.'

'Well, you were right. And now, I insist you walk me there like the gallant man you are.'

'A romance for Watson? Surely not.'

'Hardly a romance is it?'

'Not the way you write it, no, more of a travelogue which is what I thought it may turn out to be.'

'What, having the odd church or painting makes it a travelogue does it?'

'If the travelling cap fits…'

'Funny man.'

'So, can we have another dead body soon?'

'How soon is soon?'

'Like now. On and what's with this Countess and her ziz and zat?

'She is exotic!'

'Hmm.'

Santa Maria Gloriosa dei Frari

Chapter Six

I walked with a keen sense of embarrassment with Emmeline clinging to my arm and whispering in my ear. I felt everyone we passed was staring at us or more particularly me. Did they see me as some kind of aging Lothario, desperate to re-discover his lost youth? I consoled myself momentarily that they may interpret what they saw as a father and daughter enjoying the delights of Venice together. If anyone observing our journey to the Hotel Vivaldi truly thought that then it is just as well they did not hear the actual words that Emmeline whispered in my ear.

My immediate concern was how to disentangle myself from her once we reached the hotel for I had not fully developed the next part of my scheme, the ultimate goal of which was to infiltrate the inner circle of the Countess. I had not worked out a strategy for so doing without being alone with Miss Cousins.

Before too long we found ourselves in *Piazza San Marco*, just a few minutes' walk away from the Vivaldi.

'Have you visited the *Palazzo Ducale?*'

'I have been meaning to.'

'Shall we go tomorrow? If you are not too tired of course.'

'Why on earth would you imagine me to be too tired?'

'Being in my company this evening may have that effect on you, John. Don't worry I will try not to tire you out too much.'

'I am afraid I have a prior engagement with my friends this evening. We are going to a...er...recital.'

She let go of my arm and turned to face me, eyes blazing. Suddenly, I thought that she would make a fearsome adversary. She fairly spat her words out.

'Your friends, your friends? Do you really want to spend time with them instead of me? Look at me, dammit, look at me.'

She thrust her body towards me, most provocatively in this most public of places.

'I am a man of my word and I cannot in all honesty cancel my engagement, but I am perfectly content to spend time with you tomorrow.'

She calmed down at those words. 'Ten o' clock tomorrow morning then. You may embrace me.'

She threw her arms around my neck and clung to me a few seconds before turning and flouncing off in the manner of a petulant child. The little amount of warmth there had been in the weak sunshine now started to cool considerably as I walked along the quayside back to the *pensione*. The traders were packing away their wares. Of Peterson's man there was no sign, but no doubt his place had been taken by another. Only then did it dawn on me that my engineered meeting with the Countess's group would in all likelihood have been observed, noted and logged. Admittedly, the officer would not have known my identity, but a description, if given to Holmes, would leave him in no doubt as to this 'mystery man'.

Holmes was at the *pensione* when I arrived, sitting in the dining-room with Grimaldi and his wife. Maria Grimaldi was stifling pitiful sobs, her husband doing his best to comfort her. Even allowing for the brief time we were in her company the previous evening, she seemed to have aged overnight. I paid my respects as best I could and Grimaldi escorted his wife from the room.

'Ah, Watson, I trust that you feel rejuvenated for having a little time to yourself.'

'I feel refreshed, Holmes, thank you. How was your day?'

'You proceed too fast, my dear fellow. I am sure your day was rather more interesting than mine.'

'I think not.'

'When a man returns from his solitary afternoon looking distinctly flushed, with a lingering aroma of an exotic perfume and two blonde hairs firmly attached to the collar of his coat then I think I am perfectly justified in deducing his day must have been interesting to say the least.'

'It was a chance encounter with an overzealous sales girl who was overly grateful for my custom. It was just one of those trivialities of life that you are so fond of, Holmes.'

'It was not a chance encounter in *Santa Maria Gloriosa Dei Frari* then?'

'The what, Holmes?'

'It won't do, it really won't do. We cannot count dissimulation among your many talents. There is a leaflet protruding from your pocket that tells me you have visited the church. Further, you have that bloated look that comes upon you when you have dined rather too well. You are far from accustomed to eating out alone especially in a foreign city. The question should be therefore; who did you meet in the *Frari*? Unless your mysterious sales girl further showed her appreciation of your custom by treating you to a meal.'

'Well...I...um...'

'Shall I tell you what I know? A report from one of those Peterson set on the tail of the Countess describes how young Emmeline fell into the company of an Englishman in the *Frari*. Whether this meeting was by design or an accident I am sure you will tell me for the description of this man fits you like a glove in every detail. The group splintering into three groups and the lack of resources available resulted in Emmeline not being tailed. The officer thought it just another tawdry amorous episode. I believe I know you better than that. All the same, an explanation is in order don't you think?'

I proceeded to take Holmes through the events of the day from the first inkling of my scheme to the parting with Miss Cousins in the *Piazzetta San Marco*. I attempted to familiarise him with my train of thought as the day had worn on.

He listened to my rambling with a stony face. Whatever emotions he was feeling did not betray themselves on his features.

'The meeting with Emmeline Cousins tomorrow cannot take place. I forbid it.'

'It is not your place to forbid it, Holmes. I am not an errant schoolboy who can be punished for misbehaving. I know what I am doing.'

'Officer Mazzini too, knew what he was doing. Have you forgotten what happened to him, how painfully he died?'

'I have not forgotten nor have I forgotten the sight of Angelo's body. It is why I have taken the action I have. I repeat, I know what am I doing and I can take care of myself.'

'I have always commended your courage, indeed there is no man I would rather have at my side, but this is foolhardy. We can take them another way.'

'My mind is made up. I have met danger before, I will not shirk from this.'

'If you are determined to go ahead then you are right, I cannot reasonably prohibit it, but we do need another of Peterson's men close by in the hotel who can liaise quickly and easily with you. You are aware of course that it is one thing to be on familiar terms with a young woman who is unaccountably infatuated with you and your *largesse*, it is quite another to be in a position to learn anything useful from the other members of Lenska's troop. I urge you to take all precautions in keeping yourself safe. One false move on your part could be fatal. Have you considered how to fend off Emmeline's advances? I assume there are lengths you will not go to and lines you will not cross.'

'You are quite right. As to how I deal with it, well, I have an idea or two. If she thinks me a man of means then that may outweigh any other consideration for her. I believe the promise of being showered in gifts and trinkets will gain me some precious time. Besides, without being indelicate, she will have no problems finding the kind of pleasure she seeks elsewhere.'

Our discussion was interrupted by the arrival of Stafford Peterson. Holmes apprised him of the recent developments.

'Have you really thought this through, Doctor?'

'Yes I have, Peterson.'

'If I were wearing my hat indoors then I would take it off to you. In fact...'

He picked up his hat which he had laid casually on one of the dining chairs, placed on his head then promptly took it off again.

'I have some news, gentlemen. Unbeknown to me the director of the *Accademia* has been seeking to make changes after a few lapses amongst his current security personnel. Any such changes should have been discussed with the *offizio culturale*, but that's by the by. He has been approached recently by two men of Middle European appearance, with impeccable credentials, who are willing to provide security at a more than reasonable rate. They have provided the director with glowing testimonials from galleries and museums throughout Europe.'

'They make their move then,' stated Holmes.

'My only concern is that it is the *Accademia* involved. If the plan is to rob it, well I don't know, from what we know about Countess Lenska it seems too well-known a target. The high profile of such a crime would surely make evading capture so much harder for them. Something about it does not add up.'

'Perhaps she intends to retire and a major theft would represent her nest egg. As for evading capture, they have been here four weeks, time enough to plot an escape route. Would they expect to be under surveillance I wonder?'

'I suspect not. They think themselves above the law and cannot be touched by it. It is only by chance that the person who organised the infiltration of her group in Florence is now in Venice. I can honestly say that were I not here than no one in the police force in Venice would be any the wiser who is in their midst. Shared intelligence between the various city forces simply does not happen.'

'If you are half the policeman I believe you to be, I assume you will have advised the director to agree to these two men taking on responsibility for the security.'

'Did I detect a compliment there, Mr Holmes?'

'If you are half the policeman I believe you to be...then you would know,' replied Holmes drily.

'Just the kind of answer I would expect from you.'

'I am always most gratified that I never disappoint you.'

'I have advised the director along those lines, yes.'

'But isn't that playing into their hands, if indeed it is them?' I asked

'Far from it,' Holmes retorted, 'it plays into our hands for it gives us the best chance against them. In fact, with this new information there is no longer a pressing case that we continue with your own plan.'

'Be that as it may, but in lieu of any hard facts I will still see it through. I will meet Emmeline at ten o' clock tomorrow as arranged and there will be no need to set a tail on us.'

'Indeed not, Doctor. Our energies will be directed elsewhere. I should however be able to offer you some support within the hotel itself. I have just come from having further words with *Vice-Questore* Rossi, who faced with a possible threat to the *Accademia* has managed to lay his hands on one or two extra men. If you should not find yourself otherwise engaged tomorrow evening I will let you know who your contact will be in the Vivaldi.'

'Thank you, I would be most grateful. Perhaps if *Vice-Questore* Rossi has any money to spare in his budget, he could consider some recompense for an impoverished doctor. I fear I may be about to stretch my own budget somewhat!'

'Somehow, I feel he would take some persuading. Beyond even my capabilities I feel.'

'Even?' queried Holmes.

'In spite of that last comment of yours, I invite you both to dine with me at a small *trattoria* where the food and company is ideal for forgetting troubles temporarily.'

'Thank you, it sounds just the ticket. I am none too sure of Watson, his waistcoat is still bearing the strain of his earlier meal.'

'Thank you for the invitation, but I fear I must decline. I am quite unable to eat another mouthful. I think I will retire early with a good book.'

'Or failing that, one of Clark Russell's interminable sea-faring adventures.'

'Clark Russell is one of my favourite authors, Doctor,' declared Peterson.

'On reflection, that does not surprise me,' Holmes remarked,

'Have you a particular favourite?' I asked.

'*The Death Ship.* I do not believe it can be bettered.'

'I am pleased to hear it for it is the volume I have with me. I found a copy of it in a bookshop in Rome.'

'I fear I am intruding. Perhaps I should dine alone and leave you two to discuss the merits of one monotonously described sea-wreck as opposed to another.'

'You are a complete Philistine at times, Holmes. Sometimes you know, a little light reading is good for the soul.'

'I beg to differ, reading something like Reade's *The Martyrdom of Man* can be accurately described as good for the soul. His insights run deep, his thrust incisive and conclusions formidable.'

'Truthfully,' I said, smiling, 'I found it as dry as...'

'Dust?'

'…no, your monographs!'

'You wound me deep. Watson. Come, Peterson, if I can tear you away from the William Clark Russell appreciation society's first meeting. Goodnight, Brutus!'

'Goodnight, Holmes. Goodnight, Peterson. I will give you my thoughts on *The Death Ship* tomorrow.'

I read long into the evening before the arms of Morpheus claimed me. The book held my interest despite the lack of sea-wrecks that Holmes seemed to think populated Russell's novels. I would account it as being one of his best books. Both in his novels and in his wonderful short stories he has set down the semblance of sea life and of the changing beauty of the waters as faithfully as such things can be done. One day I would force Holmes to sit down and read one.

When I came down to breakfast Holmes was already seated in the dining-room. I glanced towards to the kitchen and could see Grimaldi hard at work in there; I would not be required this morning to exercise my domestic skills.

'You are safe this morning, Watson. Maria is in there too. I think you will agree that following a normal routine may be of great benefit to her now.'

'I do agree.'

'Are you apprehensive about your day?'

'I will confess to feeling so, yes.'

'As we said yesterday, there is no necessity for you to continue. No one, least of all myself will think any the worst of you.'

'My mind is made up. What will you be doing?'

'I will be visiting the *Accademia* along with Peterson. We will encourage the director to arrange a time with our gentlemen friends so that we may be in attendance.'

'Won't they think it odd?'

'Peterson is the head of the *offizio culturale* and would be expected to be involved. I will be presented as his assistant.'

'They may know your name, Holmes.'

'Which is why, rather like yourself, I will be employing an alias. Now, Watson, I urge you to show caution today, be vigilant. We are dealing with people who set no great store on the sanctity of human life.'

'Most of my time will be spent with Miss Cousins who, although I have seen a momentary dark side, is actually very sweet in spite of her loose morals. I cannot believe she knows anything of these murders; she is also in need of rescue.'

'You have no white charger, Watson, much less the data you need to reach a verdict on what Miss Cousins knows or does not know.'

'I believe I am a good judge of character, Holmes.'

'I take a contrary view. Your weakness is always to see or attempt to see the good in everybody.'

'Is that necessarily a weakness?'

'Indeed, for you are blinded to faults that the reasoned observer will see as obvious. You own innate goodness can often be your undoing. All I say is, delay judgment on Miss Cousins. These are deep waters and she may be a long way out from the shallows.'

'I will endeavour to keep my wits about me.'

Grimaldi arrived with our breakfast which I toyed with absent-mindedly and finally pushed away from me.

My appetite was gone.

8694. P. Z - VENEZIA. RIVA SCHIAVONI E STA. MARIA DELLA SALUTE.

'You're making this up as you go along aren't you?'
'Obviously.'
'Any idea what will happen?'
'None at all.'
'I have an idea, but only because I find you a little predictable, mate!'
'What's your idea?'
'Watson fall for Emmeline. Rescues her from the baddies. Divorces what's her face…and lives happily ever after.'
'That's what you honestly think is it?'
'Guessing it's better than whatever you will come up with. Talking about guessing…are we getting a guided tour of the Doges' palace now?

Chapter Seven

I elected to leave the *pensione* much earlier than I needed to in order to stretch my legs and collect my thoughts. I walked out into bright sunshine, the lagoon positively twinkled and shimmered. I took a perambulatory route which took me past the *Arsenale* and would eventually bring me to the eastern end of the *Piazza San Marco* in plenty of time to get to the Vivaldi provided I did not lose my way completely.

The whole city seemed alive with sparkle and sunshine, the sky a vibrant shade of blue. An air of freedom pervaded the city as if it had been granted life by the morning sun. Every alleyway, every square was light, spacious and carefree in a way denied by the rain clouds. Venice could in fact now show itself off, a city that lives for flattery like a capricious and knowing lady. No wonder Venetians and tourists alike come out in their droves to celebrate the city once the damp miasma lifts.

While I crossed a bridge a short distance from the *Piazza*, I was amused to see a quarrel between two gondoliers. Whether this was about territory, moorings or customers I could not tell. The argument raged in a series of crescendos and deflations as each one tried to gain the ascendancy over the other. At one of these apexes one of the protagonists walked away, seemingly resigned to defeat, but he suddenly turned and advanced on his rival with much abuse. The argument continued sporadically thus before it rose in pitch once more and the voices became louder and shriller. When for the world I was expecting them to come to blows, there was suddenly a handshake and they strolled away together like the best of friends.

The *Piazza* was bathed in a golden light and was already very busy indeed. The square acts like a magnet drawing visitors under its spell. Making my way to the *Piazzetta* and walking past the *Palazzo Ducale* I halted to gaze at the Bridge of Sighs, for some who were shepherded through it, it may have been their last sight of Venice before being incarcerated in the darkness of the city prisons. No wonder they would sigh.

It was now just a few minutes before ten o' clock and I elected to wait inside the hotel. It was the very height of luxury and I dread to think what monies one would have to part with to stay within its hallowed portals. If it can be decreed fashionable for ladies to be late for appointments then I can truly say that Miss Emmeline Cousins was very fashionable indeed.

'I hope you haven't been waiting too long, John. I spent extra care making sure I looked my very best for you.'

'No, not too long at all. The extra care was worth it from what I can see.'

'You are too kind.'

'Are you alone?'

'Of course. I have no need of a chaperone. I am a grown woman now or had you not noticed?'

I fear I blushed once more, it was becoming a regular occurrence when in Emmeline's company.

'That was not my meaning. I have become used to seeing you with the others of your group.'

'Shall I go and get them, if you rather see them? I am sure they would be thrilled to see you.'

'I am more than happy with you and you alone, Emmeline. Come along, take my arm...the *Palazzo Ducale* awaits.'

Reluctantly, she did so, but I was aware that it was all just so much play-acting on her part. Rather as I could with Holmes, I could imagine Miss Cousins gracing the stage.

'Are you going to buy me a magnificent lunch today? I went without breakfast in anticipation.'

'Certainly. I ensured I brought sufficient funds for if I may say so, you have a very healthy appetite.'

'In all things, John,' she responded, laughing.

There was a small group ahead of us awaiting patiently admittance to the palace. They chattered amongst themselves in a language I did not recognise, possibly a Slavonic tongue according to

Emmeline. We amused ourselves for the next ten minutes putting our own interpretations to the unfamiliar words they spoke.

I think it to be no more than the truth when I say the splendour of the *Palazzo Ducale* will always stay with me. From the impressive ceremonial stairway, the *Scala Dei Giganti* to the *Sala de Collegio* and from the meeting room of the Council of Ten, the *Sala Dei Consiglio Dei Dieci* to the great council chamber, the *Sala Dei Maggior Consiglio*, it held me in thrall. I had quite simply never seen anything to compare with it. The state rooms were awash with the work of some of the very finest Venetian painters. Perhaps the most notable of these was Tintoretto's *Paradiso* which for sheer size and scope could hardly be surpassed. It covers the whole of one end wall of the great council chamber. The size can be imagined by the knowledge this one chamber could hold an assembly of two thousand, five hundred souls, all busy debating state policies.

'Impressive isn't it?'

'It is certainly that, Emmeline.'

'How many figures would you say are in the painting?'

I peered closely and walked up and down in front of it, scrutinising. Counting was an exercise in futility, but I came up with what I considered a reasonable estimate.

'Two hundred and fifty,' I ventured.

'The actual figure is *three* hundred and fifty. Quite a feat for a man in his seventies although he did have the assistance of his son.'

'It is magnificent.'

'Do you see up there?' asked Emmeline, pointing towards the ceiling. 'There are portraits which line the cornice. There you can see the features of seventy-six doges. Follow the line along, John, what do you see?'

'There is a gap between the paintings with just a black veil to fill it.'

'It is the intended place of honour of the 14th century Doge, Marin Falier. It is his lot to be publicly disgraced and eternally shamed in this manner.'

'What fate befell him?'

'He was beheaded for treason in 1355.'

'You are very knowledgeable.'

'And that surprises you?'

'No, I just find it unusual in a young woman like yourself.'

'I am passionate when it comes to art as I am in other areas. Do you think the fact I shock you with my forwardness betrays a lack of intelligence? Why should I not be as knowledgeable as an oh so proper lady?'

'You must forgive me, I did not mean to cast aspersions on your character or your intelligence.'

'I am pleased to hear it. You may take me to the dungeons now!'

Our route to the dungeons took us through the Bridge of Sighs. Miss Cousins disabused me of the notion that it was so-called because of the sighs of condemned prisoners as they caught their last sight of Venice before their final incarceration since she told me that by the time the bridge was built it was only petty criminals who would be making that journey.

'Shall I choose the restaurant?' she asked as we exited the palace into the *piazzetta.*

I feared grave repercussions for my wallet if I allowed it, but I had little choice. I had to go along with it. I followed her towards *Dorsoduro* once more. After we crossed the *Ponte Accademia* we turned abruptly right and her destination was revealed; a very expensive looking eatery, *La Cicolina.* It was obviously very popular judging by the number of diners present.

A waiter of mature years hurried across to us. *'E al completo.'*

'Mi chiamo, Emmeline.' She motioned him to bend slightly and she whispered something in his ear, causing him to redden.

He walked away and then reappeared beckoning us to follow him. We were shown to a small private dining area.

'Ecco.'

'Cosa mi consiglia?' Emmeline asked.

He proceeded to take us through the menu dish by dish, his recommendations or otherwise were accompanied my much gesturing. I settled for *fegato alla Veneziana,* served with polenta. Emmeline, after deliberating for ten minutes, decided on *Anguilla alla Veneziana.*

'How long will you remain in Venice? Does Countess Lenska intend to move on?'

'She has not said and I have not asked. To be honest, I have grown a little tired of her company. She lives for pleasure, living off others, devouring their flattery. Of course I am grateful to her for taking me under her wing, but the time has come for me to stand on my own two feet.'

'Do Marguerite and Anna feel as you do?'

'I do not care what they think. They must do as they like. Lev and Yev likewise. We are none of us friends, not really.'

'Lev and Yev, those are their names?'

'Shortened versions of their given names. They are brothers from Ukraine. Just lately they scare me. Oh, I'm sure they would do me no harm, but all the same I feel a little intimidated.'

'Are they violent men?'

'No, John, at least I do not think so. There was an incident recently though, no, it was nothing...'

'I would like to hear, Emmeline.'

'Like I say, it was nothing and I'm probably reading too much into what I heard. The Countess has been favouring the company of a gondolier recently. He was often at the hotel entertaining and being entertained. She thought him a skilled lover. For his part, he was happy enough to do his duty and receive his cash and gifts which she showered on him. I think it was three nights ago when I heard raised voices. The Countess shouted for Lev and Yev to come to her apartment. It was shortly after that when I heard what sounded like a cry of pain, followed by a single scream.'

'What leads you to think it is connected to this gondolier?'

'He was at the hotel every day. John, I have not seen him since.'

'You must go the authorities, tell them what you know.'

'It was nothing. He probably just got tired of her demands and is out there somewhere on his gondola, serenading tourists.'

I was very tempted at that moment to come clean as to who I was and what I already knew about Angelo. Miss Cousins could be just the kind of witness that Holmes, Peterson and various continental police forces would welcome. I decided, however, to stay my hand for a while, but saw nothing wrong in telling Emmeline of the discovery of the body, leaving out my appearance at the scene.

'The body of a gondolier was pulled from a canal yesterday morning. He had been stabbed and possibly tortured.'

'Oh my god. How do you know this?'

'The owner of the *pensione* I am staying at, told me all about it. It features in all the papers this morning. That is why it is important to reveal what you know even if you think it trivial.'

'I wouldn't like to get Lev and Yev into trouble.'

'But they may be killers, Emmeline.'

'The gondolier found in the canal may not even be the gondolier who was at the hotel. I promise you I will think about it though. Oh,' she sighed, 'everything is so different now. The Countess is more secretive, they all are. I very often walk into a room and find them all falling silent at my arrival like they are plotting something and do not wish me to hear.'

'Do you suspect them of that?'

'Of what?'

'Of plotting.'

'What on earth would they be plotting? It was just an expression, John, nothing more.'

The waiter appeared with our meals. The calf's liver looked a little under cooked and I wished I had decided on the eels also.

'*Ecco, buon appetito.*'

Emmeline displayed the same healthy appetite as before and I had hardly half-finished my meal she was busy mopping up the remnants of her sauce with some particularly crusty bread.'

'You'll have to hurry, John, otherwise I'll be ordering dessert alone!'

I gracefully declined dessert which only served to persuade Emmeline that she should in fact eat two. Once she had demolished the *tiramisu* followed by *panna cotta* she became eager to show me more of Venice. I put off asking for the bill as long as I could, but the moment had arrived.

'*Mi porta il conto, per favore.*'

'My, your Italian is getting better John. You have hidden talents...I hope.'

The extortionate bill having been duly paid, Emmeline announced she was taking me to the church of *Santa Maria Della Salute*. I was familiar to an extent with the exterior given that it commands such a massive presence at the entrance of the Grand Canal.

I confess I was a little disappointed with the interior, expecting it to be as equally magnificent as the exterior. There was of course the obligatory Tintoretto, in this case a wonderfully composed *Marriage at Cana* and three more Biblical paintings by Titian. Emmeline informed me that over one million oak pilings were sunk into the swampy earth to support the structure.

The sunshine was still out-manoeuvring the forecast grey cloud when we left the church. We walked back towards the *Ponte Accademia* at a leisurely pace. As we approached the *Accademia* itself I saw Holmes and Peterson standing on the steps of its entrance. Involuntarily, I nodded. Emmeline noticed my movement.

'Who are you nodding to?' she asked.

'I thought I saw my friends, but I was mistaken.'

'Are they good friends of yours?'

'Yes, they are.'

'Yet you have trouble telling them apart from strangers. How odd.'

'Well, it was only a fleeting glimpse and the sun was in my eyes,' I offered weakly.

'Take a good look at me, John and try and remember me for tomorrow. Come now, I'm only teasing. Let's go back to the Vivaldi. You may buy me a glass of wine.'

When we arrived at the hotel, Emmeline ordered a bottle of wine to be delivered to the fifth floor where her room was situated. As we ascended the plushly carpeted stairs Emmeline was hailed from the reception area.

'Who is zat with you, Emmeline?'

'It is John. You met him yesterday,' she replied curtly.

'Ah, yes. My apologies, Mister...'

'Williams, Countess Lenska.'

'Zat is zo yes. Come and join us for afternoon tea. Very English.'

I was not sure whether to be relieved or not, reflecting on the old proverb regarding frying pans and fires, but refusal did not seem to be an option. Emmeline glared at the Countess in open defiance, but to no avail.

Emmeline's displeasure deepened all the more when Marguerite and Anna joined me on the settee in the Countess's suite.

'You haf been kind to Miss Cousins, yes?' asked the Countess.

'He has,' interjected Emmeline. 'He has bought me lunch twice now,' she said, giggling like a schoolgirl instead of the intelligent woman I knew her to be. Perhaps the Countess gained some perverse pleasure from keeping those in her entourage utterly subservient.

'I trust you haf a full wallet. Ze thing that Emmeline likes most of all in zis world is a man that spends money on her. Trust me....you will haf your reward. Oh yes,' she said, laughing with everyone in the room joining in.

Emmeline jumped up from her seat and pulled me to my feet in spite of Marguerite and Anna endeavouring to hold on me.

'Come, John. We will go to my room.'

This was greeted with more laughter and what I took for obscene gestures from Lev and Yev.

When we reached her room, Emmeline locked the door, embraced and began immediately to disrobe. In spite of the manifest charms of this bewitching creature, I kept my resolve.

'There is something I have to tell you,' I said, as she pulled me to her. 'I have...er...a medical condition which means...er...that I cannot...'

'What?' she queried in a voice that surely all of Venice heard. 'What?'

'It's true I am afraid.'

'So, you don't find me attractive?'

'It's not that. You are a lovely woman and I have enjoyed your company immensely. Perhaps I could treat you to another meal tomorrow or maybe take a boat out to one of the islands. I have wired my bank for extra funds that are due to me after a recent investment paid dividends.'

'How much of a dividend?' she asked as she hurriedly dressed.

I thought of a figure quickly. 'Ten thousand pounds.'

'Let's drink that wine now,' she said, her scowl replaced by a smile.

'Poor Watson!'

'How do you mean?'

'A medical condition…honestly!'

'Had to think of something to keep him from Emmeline's clutches. Anyway, he's a doctor, he can cure himself.'

'If he is not too busy gazing at paintings. Tintoretto's all over the place, mate.'

'He was a busy man.'

'Obviously. Is the Countess supposed to be speaking with a Russian accent? I mean, do you think chucking in the odd zis or zat is going to work?'

'It's still vaguely exotic.'

'It's not vaguely anything, mate.'

Chapter Eight

I was under no illusions that the attraction I held for Emmeline was more to do with a matter of finances, but that was what I wanted. In spite of her mercenary ways, she was most pleasant indeed and the fact she wanted her independence from the Countess could help bring Angelo's killers to justice. When I left her she was sleeping, the wine having rendered her weary in the extreme. Before she succumbed to sleep she promised that she would do her very best to recall exactly what happened that final night Angelo was at the Vivaldi. I hoped she would do the right thing, but it had to be her decision.

'Watson!'

'Hullo, Holmes, Peterson.'

They both looked very relaxed, sipping wine in the late afternoon sunshine seated outside a small tavern.

'Would you care for a glass of this very fine white, Watson? Although I fear you have over-indulged already judging by your flushed face.'

'I may have had a glass or two…to be social and keep Miss Cousins company.'

'You are a gentleman indeed, Doctor!'

'Thank you, Peterson. Did you arrange things satisfactorily at the *Accademia*?'

'We were fortunate indeed for our quarry arrived there only thirty minutes after us. We were in the throes of trying to arrange such a meeting at the very moment they were admitted. There was however a small difficulty, one we had not foreseen.'

'To be perfectly honest, it was an eventuality that I had considered.'

'Really, Peterson. Only you can couple the words 'perfectly honest' with an audacious lie.'

'Not just me I am sure.'

'As you say. I merely take the opportunity once again to point out that I do not always take your word as gospel.'

'I was going to utter exactly the same words.'

'I apologise for interrupting your flow, but could one of you explain the small difficulty you encountered?'

'The two men who we met were not the two men in Lenska's entourage.'

'Not Lev and Yev?'

'Excellent, Watson. You have acquired names to put to those two memorable faces. I am glad to see that your day has not been given over solely to Bacchanalian feasts. No, our pair proved to be Hungarian and as far as we could ascertain they are respected businessmen. All their papers and testimonials were in order and they displayed no alarm at finding us ensconced with the director.'

'They answered all our questions.' Peterson added, 'with no hesitation at all.'

'Perhaps they are in league with the Countess. Being respected businessmen is no barrier to greed after all.' I ventured.

'In order to bring matters to a head we asked the director to compile a list of the twenty most valuable paintings in the collection. We can be reasonably sure some of them at least would be on the shopping list of any would be thief. We explained to our Hungarian friends that these twenty paintings were being moved to a temporary exhibition and they would be leaving the morning after tomorrow. The director made it clear the he was dissatisfied with his current security officers and could they take up their duties tomorrow evening. They talked it over and acquiesced.'

'A trap then, Holmes.'

'Indeed, but not one necessarily that anyone will fall into. If they do then we will strike. We will be admitted to the building tomorrow evening before the new security team come in at eight o' clock. It may be that we will have a wasted evening. Equally so, we may find we have a full net to show for our trawling. Now, Watson, it is time we heard the events of your day.'

I recounted for them both the conversations I had held with Emmeline in particular of course, what she overheard the night of Angelo's disappearance.

'One can only hope she sees sense because while Lev and Yev may be prepared to suffer a short spell in gaol for minor demeanours with promises of riches to come if they keep quiet, but faced with a noose one supposes they will not be inclined to suffer alone. When do you see her next?'

'Tomorrow afternoon. She informs me she has hair and clothes fitting appointments to keep which will render her busy until then at the very least.'

'There seems very little we can do until that time.'

'I think out of courtesy we should inform Professor Collins of Angelo's death.'

'He will know of it already. Officers of the *polizia locale* would have been despatched to Angelo's apartment and questioned his neighbours.'

'I have no doubt, but all the same he may appreciate hearing about it from us.'

'Very well, that will be our plan for the morning. You look as though something else is troubling you.'

'Frankly, it puzzles me that someone like the Countess who from all accounts is extremely well-known can evade detection for this amount of time.'

'It may be precisely because of her fame that she has been able to operate in the way she does. Those in the highest strata of society very often imagine themselves above the law and accordingly. After at least twenty years of being at the hub of continental high society I imagine Lenska considers herself completely safe and secure.'

'Indeed,' agreed Peterson, 'although the rumours regarding her lifestyle and how it is funded have been a more recent development, five or six years actually. We, as I have said, know very little about her. She may be Russian, she may not. She may be titled, she may not. Does she have a fortune at her disposal? We do not know. Has she ever been married? We have no idea.'

'Hungary!' I cried.

'After the lunch you described to us, Watson? Surely not!'

'No. Hungary...the country!'

'What of it?'

'You say the two men you met at the *Accademia* are Hungarian. Miss Cousins told me that she first met the Countess in Budapest some six years ago. A connection do you think?'

'Of sorts yes. What was Miss Cousins doing in Budapest? Did she inform you?'

'I believe she was actively involved in spending the last few pounds of her late husband's fortune. Is that useful to us though?'

'Everything is of use. All these facts can be docketed away until such time that we can see their relation to each other and in the meantime, you are still finding the time to enjoy Venice in the company of a lovely young woman.'

'I never tire of Venice even though my schedule allows little time for relaxation.'

'My dear Peterson, you appear to me to be perfectly relaxed.'

'Maybe a tad so,' Peterson replied, draining his glass. 'If I could find myself an assistant, one I am desperately in need of, I would be considerably more so. How about it, Mr Holmes? Come and join me here.'

'To be your assistant?'

'Well, if the deerstalker fits!'

'The idea does have its merits you will be surprised to hear.'

'Nothing you say or do surprises me. You may interpret that how you wish.'

'I have done so I assure you. As much as it may be an interesting option for me I fear I would have to refuse. By this time next year I will be retired.'

'Retired!' I spluttered, 'what do you mean, retired?'

'I use the word in its traditional sense, Watson. That is to say, I will no longer be in gainful employment.'

'I do not understand, Holmes.'

'I could have not made it any clearer.'

'Why would you want to turn your back on your career? Your name is known throughout Europe as the greatest detective of the age. You are the last court of appeal, the highest to the humblest see you as the champion of the law and the scourge of the lawless.'

'I believe Doctor Watson has a point despite the obvious flattery. Of course, knowing you well, he is aware of your susceptibility to such flattery. Surely though, it is premature to speak of retirement.

You are still a comparatively young man although admittedly older than me. By some years.'

'Hardly young, Peterson. Forty-eight is well into middle-age by anyone's reckoning. And I recognise that you are indeed the younger man. After all, your immaturity shines like a beacon. Simply, I have grown tired of this life I created for myself. The great criminals have gone and the great cases along with them. All I see is mediocrity and a lack of ingenuity. I am no longer challenged, gentlemen.'

'Is the most important thing you being challenged? Should it not rather be helping others?' I asked rather coldly.

'Whatever my skills as a detective may be, and I leave that for others to judge, those skills are considerably heightened by the more abstruse a problem may be. You have taken the Hippocratic Oath, Watson. You are duty bound to help others yet there will come a time when you too will wish to retire. I do not propose to spend my time doing nothing. I have some aims, some ambitions.'

'I have a question,' Peterson announced.

'I rather thought you might,' Holmes responded drily.

'Shall I order some more wine?'

We nodded, even though I was wary that my intake was approaching its limit.

'*Scusi*, he called. '*Vorrei il bottiglia vino rosso, per favore.*'

'May I ask what these aims and ambitions are Holmes?'

'You may indeed, Watson. I intend to write the definitive book on the art of detection. A work which will encompass every facet of detective work, a handbook if you like. Everything I have learned and put to practical use will be within its pages.'

'It will be quite a thin volume then,' Peterson offered.

'Your wit can be most trying at times.'

'So I believe. It encourages me all the more.'

'I will also keep bees.'

'What?' I asked, spluttering once more. 'Bees? I was not aware you had an affinity for the creatures.'

'Bees are fascinating and complex. Do you not think so?'

'I have to say, Holmes that I have not given them much thought. When do you intend to put all this into operation?'

'Spring of next year seems the ideal time for a fresh beginning. My plans are well under way.'

'Where will you retire to? I cannot imagine hives in the rear yard of 221b.'

'There is no need to imagine it, Watson. I have been casting my eye over properties in Sussex, specifically the downs that stretch down to Beachy Head where there are glorious views over the Channel.'

'It's not a situation I can imagine you in. After all, I know very well your views on the countryside; you have never been inclined towards painting a rosy picture of life outside the city.'

'That was more to do with the impunity with which crimes may be committed there rather than a verdict on the countryside itself. I appreciate beauty as much as the next man and when it comes down to it you cannot beat nature for beauty. Perhaps it is time for me to concentrate on the mysteries of nature.'

'Have you the funds to enable you to cease work fully if it is not too indelicate a question?'

'It is not a recent decision. I have been saving and working towards this goal for six years. Hmm, six years. It seems to be the common theme this evening. Six years since Miss Cousins met Countess Lenska. Six years since the Countess was in Hungary and six years since, according to you Peterson, that her criminal career began or at least suspicions and rumours arose.'

'According to me, Mr Holmes? You make me sound untrustworthy.'

'Well, if the *capello* fits!'

'Is the six years significant?' I asked.

'Let's just say for now that it is of interest. Its significance or otherwise may yet become apparent.'

'If you find retirement does not suit, my offer will still be standing. You have the makings of a fine policeman.'

'Thank you, Peterson, I wish I could say the same regarding you, but alas...'

'What happens tomorrow night if...nothing happens?' I asked.

'We still have the possibility that Miss Cousins will be willing to testify as to what she heard.'

'And if she is not willing for whatever reason?'

'Then we will have to formulate a new direction to go in.'

'And you still maintain it would be of no use whatsoever to detain Lev and Yev and put pressure on them?'

'Mr Holmes is right to think we would get nothing from them in that situation. Emmeline's testimony may make them think twice. I think we should perhaps stop shadowing the whole group tomorrow night should any or all of them leave the hotel. The last thing we want to do is spook them. By the way, Doctor, the man I have placed in the hotel is Beppo. He will make himself known to you, discreetly of course.'

'Thank you, Peterson. I fear my head is beginning to spin; the wine has taken its toll. I will head back to the *pensione* for some much needed rest. I will see you tomorrow, Peterson. Goodbye for now. Good evening, Holmes.'

'You don't think all this retirement talk is a bit strained, mate?'
'If I did it wouldn't be there would it?'
'The point is...is there any point to it?'
'Of course.'
'What? This six years thing. Was that the point?'
'Maybe. Besides, it's 1902 and Holmes retired the following year. People might like to know what was in his mind.'
'He wasn't real, mate!'

Chapter Nine

I elected to take an early morning walk to clear my head. Either the wine was stronger than I thought or the passing years had weakened by ability to consume alcohol with no ill-effect.

I gave some thought to Holmes's revelation of the previous evening. Whilst not begrudging him his well-earned rest, I felt a little sad that a part of my life would end too. Admittedly, meeting, courting and marrying Beatrice had given fresh impetus to my life, but even so I still wholeheartedly enjoyed my comradeship and adventures with Holmes. Of late there had been few occasions when I could offer any real assistance and to some extent Holmes had come to see me as one of his institutions rather than a valued friend. I was as familiar to him as his violin, the Persian slipper or his 'good old index'. That did not negate in any way my feelings towards the man; he, for me, remained the best and wisest man I had ever known and a constant in my life for over twenty years.

There were then, two factions at war in my head. Part of me wished him well and a long and happy retirement. The other side of the coin betrayed my selfishness in wanting the *status quo* to remain. My association with Holmes had brought much that was good into my life, it had enriched it immeasurably. I did not doubt that our friendship would continue, perhaps even deepen, but Holmes was synonymous with adventure, derring-do and mystery. To imagine all that disappearing from my life was a hard cross to bear. The decision was his though and I had no right to question it; the man had done enough in his long career and if anyone deserved to live out his remaining years how he wished then it was Sherlock Holmes.

The *Piazza San Marco* was coming to life, tables being put out, areas being swept and a few souls entering the *basilica*. The sun was making its presence known although the dark clouds rolling in suggested rain was not far off. I hurried along the quayside in a valiant attempt to reach the *pensione* ahead of the rain, but the heavens opened as I turned into the *Via Garibaldi*. There was precious little cover to be obtained and in spite of my running the remaining distance I entered the building soaked to the skin.

After changing into a new set of clothes I headed down to the breakfast area where I found Holmes enjoying a pipe before eating.

'Good morning, Watson. I trust my announcement did not disorder you too much.'

'Morning, Holmes. I won't deny it was a shock.'

'The day had to come when I reckoned it was time to bring down the curtain.'

'Of course, I didn't expect it to be just yet though. You are in the prime of your career, Holmes.'

'You are very kind to say so, but I fear the truth is that my powers are on the wane. I notice it daily. I do not wish to wait and see how far down this decline in my mental faculties will bring me. That is why I propose to act sooner rather than later.'

'Then, I wish you well my dear fellow.'

'Thank you. First though we have our Venice mystery to clear up.'

'One thing puzzles me.'

'Just one, Watson?' Holmes asked, chuckling.

'If Peterson has had a man in the hotel and we accept the premise that Angelo was murdered in the Vivaldi then how were they able to remove the body unseen?'

'For one thing it's a sizeable building for one man to watch and for another they did not march through the main reception area with their cargo. You may not have noticed, but there are narrow subsidiary canals which criss-cross the city connecting to the main canals. One of these runs behind the Vivaldi, the hotel's service entrance is located there. I suggest that was their method of extraction.'

'Presumably Peterson's man being a Venice man would know of the service entrance. How come he did not spot them?'

'How indeed? Are you confident Miss Cousins will agree to testify against Lev and Yev?'

'I believe she will. She wishes to extricate herself from the Countess's clutches; this may be the best way to achieve it. Do you suppose that if she has been guilty of any offence herself that it could be overlooked in return for her testimony?'

'I am sure Peterson will look kindly on her if she cooperates even though his hands may be tied somewhat by the Venetian authorities.'

'As I recall, that did not stop you and Peterson from conspiring to conceal the identity of one of the co-conspirators in Florence. An action that the Florentine authorities would scarcely have approved of.'

'The circumstances were a little different. I am sure that if Miss Cousins does her duty then it will go all the better for her.'

The rain had cleared by the time we left to walk once more to the *Campo dei Mori* to visit Professor Collins. Holmes suggested we take a circuitous route to avoid watchful eyes, should there be any, at the Vivaldi.

We diverted, at Holmes's suggestion, to the church of *San Giovanni e Paulo*. It is most commonly known as simply *San Zanipolo*; names are often slurred together in the Venetian dialect. It shares one attribute with sister church the *Frari*; it is cavernous. The church contains the remains of twenty-five doges and various other dignitaries. It was another welcome diversion in a city where there are such diversions around every corner.

Professor Collins was surprised to see us and invited us in to his jumbled sitting-room once more. Although he had already received the news of Angelo's murder he was shocked by the details we supplied.

'Angelo was such a blazing light. It's a tragedy when such a man is cut down in his prime when God sees fit to preserve a fossil like me. Life is unfair, Mr Holmes.'

'There is a randomness to life which means the tragedies we all endure bear no pattern or design. I, for one would question what part God plays in the proceedings. For better or worse we stand on our own two feet.'

'Is there no design in the universe then?'

'We term it so, but is it really so? The same randomness we see in life is just a reflected view of the universe where we decree there must be a creator because we cannot comprehend how it could all have come about without some grand celestial plan. Our destinies are not shaped for us by a Supreme Being much less by distant planets and stars.'

'I can see you are a man who has pondered upon these matters long and hard. I have just blundered through life wrapped up in my own subjects. Whichever we look at it, it is a tragedy that befell Angelo. And now, I fear I must become inhospitable for I have a student due. Thank you for coming, gentlemen. I will look forward to reading more of your work, Doctor Watson and I trust you did not take offence at my constructive criticism.'

'Doctor Watson is used to criticism, Professor, it is like water off a duck's back to him. Goodbye.'

'It seems everyone has an opinion on my writing,' I said, as we left the apartment.

'Perhaps you should pen a letter, outlining your grievances and post it in the lion's mouth. Look on the bright side, not every opinion is a negative one.'

'You are right of course. I do have my admirers who are...'

'...easily pleased?'

'Kind enough to take time out of their day to write me occasional letters telling me how much they have enjoyed my chronicling of your adventures.'

'And they do this of their own free will?'

'You may mock, Holmes, but we have both benefited from my published accounts.'

'I do not deny it. Indeed, I have never denied it. I may have from time to time decried the lack of detail when it comes to describing the actual work of detection, but I appreciate the fact that you tell a tale well even if your prose at times is a tad too flowery for my taste.'

'Thank you.'

'Shall we find ourselves a coffee shop, somewhere off the beaten track maybe?'

After a time spent in enjoyable wandering we entered a small establishment in *Calle Della Locanda*. Not only was the coffee there quite simply the best I have ever tasted, but the mouth-watering selection of *tramezzini* was huge, containing all manner of fillings.

We spent a full hour in there discoursing on subjects as diverse as the Pyramids of Egypt, folk tales of England, the postal system and the future of the telephone.

'I'll show you something so many tourists never see, Watson,' Holmes said as I paid our bill. 'It is not easy to find, but fortunately we are on its doorstep.'

'Nothing in Venice is easy to find,' I observed.

I followed Holmes into *Calle Vida* and from there immediately into *Calle Contarini*. We turned into the smallest of alleyways and on my right was a most extraordinary sight. A *palazzo*, not large by any standards, but with a graceful spiral staircase attached to it. Arcaded and romantic, it should rightly belong in a fairy tale.

'The *Palazzo Contarini del Bovolo*,' announced Holmes. 'The staircase has its own name, *Scala del Bovolo*. *Bovolo* means 'snail-shell' in Venetian dialect and is a fitting description you will agree.'

'One of those small wonders of the city that can be stumbled across by accident. Tucked away like this, it is not surprising that it is missed by so many.'

'If we retrace our steps into the *calle* and turn right, would you be able to tell me where we end up?'

'I would hazard a guess we would arrive shortly in the *Piazza*.'

'Upon my word, Watson, you are coming to grips with the city wonderfully well. You are correct.'

'I feel very much at home here and am enjoying its nooks and crannies.'

'Isn't that Miss Cousins over there at the foot of the *campanile*?' asked Holmes as we strode across the square.

I followed his gaze. Emmeline looked up and barely raising her hand in acknowledgment, walked quickly away and was lost amongst the groups of people in the *Piazzetta dei Leoncini*.

'Odd, Holmes, she had the expression of a naughty schoolgirl having been discovered doing something she shouldn't be.'

'It may be that she has another liaison ongoing in addition to her entanglement with you. You could always ask her later.'

'I do not think so, it is hardly any of my business where she goes or who she sees.'

We parted shortly after that. Holmes was meeting up with Peterson and I, feeling unaccountably tired, returned to the *pensione* to attempt to nap. Before we went our separate ways I arranged to meet Holmes and Peterson at the *Accademia* by seven o' clock at the latest.

At the *pensione* I penned a letter to Beatrice, extolling the virtues of Venice, before sleep overtook me. I awoke with a start in the midst of a vivid dream and found it was already three o' clock. I straightened my clothes, laced up my shoes and set off for the Hotel Vivaldi.

'Are we nearly there yet?'
'Where?'
'The end! Let's have some action, mate.'
'You want action?'
'Yes I do. No more galleries or churches and Tintoretto. Action!'
'I'll see what I can do.'
'I won't hold my breath.'

Chapter Ten

I was hailed by Countess Lenska as soon as I entered the hotel. She was sitting in the lounge area which was adjacent to the reception desk. She was flanked by Marguerite and Anna.

'John, please to come and join us. Emmeline will be here soon I am sure.'

'Thank you, Countess. And *bonjour* ladies.'

'Such impeccable manners you English. We will haf afternoon tea, yes?'

'That would be delightful. Where is Miss Cousins may I ask?'

'With zat girl, who knows? She is a mystery zat one, but you haf new friends here, John.'

Marguerite and Anna were once again far too attentive, especially so as we were in a public place. I saw their smiles replaced by scowls and turning around I saw the reason for their displeasure; Emmeline had just entered the hotel. I stood up, took two steps towards her in greeting when I came face to face with Cardinal Roselli.

'Doctor Watson, how lovely to run into you again. How is Sherlock Holmes? Is he here with you?' he asked, looking around.

'I am afraid you have mistaken me for someone else, sir,' I said, hoping he would get the message I was trying to convey.

'I do not understand. What game are you playing here?'

'As I say, you are mistaking me for this...Watson...was it?'

Realisation dawned on the Cardinal's face at last.

'I am so sorry. I can see now I am in error. I do not know the doctor well, but I realise he is not as stocky as you.'

'Think nothing of it. We all make mistakes.'

The whole of the Countess's entourage had been following the exchange and I hardly dare look at them for fear my face would betray me. Emmeline whispered something in Lev's ear and he and his brother walked to the stairs.

'Where haf you been, Emmeline? You haf kept John waiting.'

'Oh I have just been gadding about,' she laughed. 'Come with me, John, there is something I need to talk to you about.'

She walked on ahead of me seemingly lost in thought. I was fervently hoping she had come to the right decision regarding what she had heard the alleged night of Angelo's disappearance.

Emmeline opened the door to her room and as I entered the room I was aware of a swift movement behind me. I had the sensation of falling from a great height with the sky gradually darkening the further I plummeted. The darkness enveloped me and my awareness came to an end.

I awoke as if from a dream, confused and disoriented. The back of my head was throbbing with a pain that ebbed and flowed in its intensity. I tried to speak, but some kind of fabric was drawn tightly across my mouth. My hands were tied behind me and my feet bound to the chair legs. I was in Emmeline's room I knew in spite of the darkness in the room. How long had I been here? Was it night? As my eyes grew accustomed to the light I could see the curtains were drawn, perhaps it was still daylight.

I was aware of voices. Lev and Yev suddenly filled my vision, muttering away to each other. There was no doubt that they were responsible for my predicament. Had they got wind of what Emmeline was planning to say to me? Where was she? What had they done with her? Lev produced a bottle and poured a little liquid onto a handkerchief, pressed it over my nose and deep sleep was once more my companion.

The sound of dripping water resounded in my head. Each drip was like the blow of a hammer amplified to almost unbearable levels. The pungent smell of chloroform filled my nostrils and I could feel the bile rising in my throat. I was strapped to a chair still, but not the same one; the texture of the surface of the wood was different under my hand. I was no longer in Emmeline's room; this was more akin to a damp, dank dungeon. I could hear lapping water. Wherever I was it was next to a canal and undoubtedly in the bowels of a building. Somewhere a door opened and closed. Muffled voices close by. The sound of a bolt being drawn back.

A small of amount light penetrated the gloom as the door opened and three figures entered. There was the sound of a match being struck and the flickering light of two candles illuminated the area immediately in front of me. Lev and Yev held a candle apiece leaving the Countess in shadow.

At a gesture from her Yev removed the gag from my mouth. I involuntarily spat bile from my mouth. The Countess took a step back and came forward, taking Yev's candle.

'Emmeline,' I gasped.

'Hello, John. I can call you John can't I? At least that part of your name is correct, Doctor Watson. A word before we start; no one can hear you. If you were to scream, which I believe you will, no one will come to your aid. Do you understand?'

I nodded, my mouth was too dry too speak.

'Good. Now, perhaps you would like to tell me where Sherlock Holmes is?'

'He is in England.'

Lev's arm came swinging out the gloom. I turned my head and the blow connected to the side of my face with such force that the chair nearly toppled to the floor.

'Shall we try again? Where is Sherlock Holmes?'

'He...he...is in Venice, but I don't know where.'

'The truth please, John.'

I shook my head in defiance and Emmeline held out her hand to Lev who placed something in it. She held it in front of my face; a knife with a thin, long blade.

'I can assure you it is very sharp. If you tell me what I need to know then you will have to make do with my assurance. If not...'

She touched my neck with the point of the blade and dragged it across my skin. I felt a trickle of blood run under my collar. My thoughts were jumbled and tempered by the fear that ran through me.

'I decided after all that you should feel the sharpness of the blade before we continue and this...'

I suffered the most excruciating pain as Lev smashed a hammer onto my knee.

'Now,' Emmeline screamed at me, 'WHERE IS SHERLOCK HOLMES?'

The door crashed open. The three of them turned towards the opening.

'I am here, Miss Cousins,' said Holmes, turning up his lantern, letting her see he was armed.

Stafford Peterson advanced on Lev and Yev, revolver in hand. They surrendered to him meekly.

'Well, Mister Sherlock Holmes. We appear to be at an impasse.'

'I do not believe that to be the case. Kindly drop the knife, Miss Cousins. I hold all the cards here.'

'This is how I see it. You are an English gentleman, you are not about to shoot a lady. Now, I estimate you are ten feet from me. The question is how quickly can you the cover the distance between us? Can you reach me before I slice open your treacherous friend's neck? Shall we see...?'

Emmeline's arm shot out, I saw the glint of the blade and as it brushed my neck there was the sound of a small explosion and Emmeline crumpled to the floor.

Holmes untied my bonds. 'Watson, a thousand apologies for not getting to you sooner. Could you attend to Miss Cousins? Peterson, could you obtain a doctor and an ambulance for our wounded souls while I cover our friends here?'

I staunched the flow of blood from a bullet hole in Emmeline's shoulder as best I could. She was just beginning to come round and even in her weakened state she was able to shoot me a look of pure hatred.

'Where am I, Holmes?' I asked, gritting my teeth as pain shot through my body.

'In the *Accademia*. Beppo got word to Peterson regarding your untimely meeting with Cardinal Roselli.'

'I thought he had withdrawn his team.'

'Save for Beppo, he had. When you failed to appear here, Peterson sent men into the Vivaldi. Missing were Miss Cousins, Lev and Yev. We were confident they were bound for the *Accademia*, but were rather less confident you were still in their company. Your scream brought us down to this ante-room.'

'The Hungarians?'

'Safely trussed upstairs. Their first action almost was to begin stripping paintings from the wall. We had begun our search of the labyrinth of rooms below the building, when as I have said, we heard you cry out.'

'I am very relieved you did.' I looked down at Emmeline. 'She really would have done it wouldn't she?'

'Yes, I am very much afraid she would. She was no doubt the prime mover behind the deaths of Angelo and Officer Mazzini. Perhaps her late husband was another victim. There may be more.'

'The Countess, what of her?'

'Blameless, I should say, at least as regards criminal activities. The last six years for Miss Cousins, one presumes, has been building to this moment, this crowning achievement to strip the *Accademia* of so many of its finest pieces. Her escape route no doubt carefully planned. Lev and Yev would be sacrificial lambs. To all intents and purposes Miss Emmeline Cousins would have no longer existed.'

'Why stay with the Countess?'

'It suited her to do so. Lenska moved in the kind of rarefied strata of society that meant rich pickings for her. And they were constantly on the move which is a boon in evading detection.'

'What of the cultivating of men like myself?'

'Amusement, pleasure, greed and pleasures of the flesh. It is how she lived her life and what motivated her.'

The pain from my knee was such that I felt myself drifting into unconsciousness. Holmes gripped my shoulder and told me help would arrive soon. I vaguely remember the trip the hospital, waking up briefly in the ambulance to be met with Emmeline's stony countenance.

'Damn you, John Watson, damn you to hell. I'll make you pay for this one day. One day...

****

I was destined to spend two weeks in hospital. I was told there was a chance I could lose my leg, but that was not the case and eventually I recovered enough mobility to enable me to be discharged into Holmes's care. A few days later we were escorted to the railway station by Stafford Peterson whose standing in the city had been considerably enhanced by his prevention of the robbery at the *Accademia* and his part in the apprehension of Angelo's killers.

I turned around on the steps for a last look at Venice. In spite of my promise to Beatrice I had the notion I would never return to the city; it had become tainted for me despite its charms and bewitching qualities.

Even so, I sometimes catch a glimpse of it in the most unexpected places as though it is around every corner. The dazzle of the city lingers in my mind. The smells, sights and sounds still fill my nostrils occasionally. The soft lapping of the back canals echo in my mind. It is always with me.

Months later we learned that Emmeline Cousins, together with the Vassilli brothers had been sentenced to thirty years hard labour for the murders of Angelo and Sandro Mazzini. They could count themselves fortunate indeed that Italy had abolished the death penalty. Their victims had had no such luck.

****

It is now 1926, a year of hardships and industrial unrest. I have seen little of Sherlock Holmes these past few years although we correspond occasionally. He penned a letter to me a few weeks ago, headed with the words: *She has been released.*

Emmeline Cousins, due to good behaviour and her great remorse had been freed from gaol with seven years of her sentence left to run, he wrote.

A week later I read a report in *The Times* detailing how wealthy socialite, Countess Lenska had been found dead in a Paris street. It was thought she had fallen from the balcony of her hotel room.

Just last week the death of a retired policeman was reported. Ordinarily it would not have merited a mention as the death occurred in Venice, but then, Stafford Peterson was a British national. The details were scarce other than to state that he was discovered in his apartment, dead from a single knife wound. Enquiries, it said, are continuing.

Holmes sent me a telegram last week, short and to the point; BE VIGILANT.

My revolver is never out of my reach. I am ready for her.

And here, as promised ››››››››››››››››››››››››

(Cue the Cuckoo Song…it's not interactive..
....you'll have to whistle it yourself!)

The Laurel and Hardy Incident

When I glance over my increasingly copious notes and records of some of the cases that my good friend, Mr Sherlock Holmes has been involved in to some degree, I am faced by a surprising amount that are out of the commonplace and present so many singular, strange features that it is no easy task for this humble chronicler to decide just which narratives to put before the public.

The incident I am about to relate involved no known crime and the puzzle, although trivial, it presented to Holmes had no solution nor in fact required one. Yet it begs to be recalled as one of those whimsical moments that can occur when six million people are jostling together in a great metropolis.

We had both broken our fast early for the heat in our Baker Street rooms was stifling. The morning sunshine bathed the street in a golden hue, the light danced and dappled its way down the thoroughfare. The morning murmur of the city coming to life was now bursting into a symphony of noise. A paean to the rich, varied life that abounds in London.

Holmes was busy reading *The Times* and I was attempting to write up the case of *The Gondolier and the Russian Countess* when we heard the doorbell, followed moments later by hurried footsteps ascending the seventeen steps.

Holmes looked up from the agony column which had been occupying his attention.

'Two men, Watson, one certainly taller and larger framed than the other, but even so just as nimble and fleet of foot as his companion.'

'I had no time to indulge Holmes's deduction with my usual 'How?' for the door opened wide and two men, such as Holmes had described entered the room. The larger of the two men, who towered over his companion was the first to speak.

'Pardon me, gentlemen for the intrusion, but we appear to be lost.'

'Yes that's right and we don't know where we are either,' announced his friend.

'You are in Baker Street,' I stated.

'Baker Street where, sir?' asked the amply proportioned one.

'In London of course. Do you not even know which city you are in?'

'London? London?' He turned to his thin friend. 'Well, here's another nice mess you've gotten me into.'

His response was to burst into tears. 'I didn't mean to...I couldn't help it....I only touched the button.'

'You can't leave anything alone can you? Pardon me, gentlemen, allow me to explain.'

'Yes, please do,' said Holmes, 'for beyond the obvious facts that you are both down on your luck, have both been in the US Navy, have bought a boat recently, have wives who hen-peck you and are regularly harassed by a balding Scotsman, I assure you I know nothing about you whatsoever.'

'Say, does this guy know us, Ollie?'

'He most certainly does not and don't call me Ollie. Gentlemen, I am Oliver Norvell Hardy and this my friend, Mr Laurel.'

'My name is Sherlock Holmes and this is my friend and colleague Doctor Watson. Now pleases explain, if you can, the nature of your predicament.'

'Well, it's like this. We were sweeping a chimney at the home of a mad scientist and he asked us not to touch a particular machine he was working on. Stanley accidentally pressed one of the buttons, pulled four levers, turned three dials and engaged six of the gears and now we find ourselves in another country.'

'I just wanted to know the time,' said Mr Laurel.

'Then why did you have to interfere with the machine?'

'He said it was a *time* machine, recomember? Say, did you say another country, Ollie? Is this London, England?'

'Why, certainly,' Mr Hardy replied.

'That's swell. I had an uncle once who was building a house in London, but he died.'

'I'm sorry to hear that Mr Laurel, what did he die of?' I asked.

105

'A Tuesday or was it a Wednesday,' he replied, taking off his hat and ruffling his hair so that it stood on end.

'No, my dear fellow. I meant what caused his death?'

'He fell through a trapdoor and broke his neck.'

'While building his house?'

'No, they were hanging him.'

I looked at Holmes intently, hoping to convey to him a silent message that one of us should make an excuse to leave and bring back the nearest constable for clearly we were in the presence of two lunatics who had escaped from Colney Hatch asylum. To my surprise, he was laughing in that peculiar silent fashion of his and was displaying no alarm at all.

'Do you have often get into scrapes like this?' he asked.

'No, I reckon this is our first mistake since that fellow sold us the Brooklyn Bridge.'

'That was no mistake, Stan. That bridge is going to be worth a lot of money to us one day.'

'Well, gentlemen,' Holmes said, his eyes twinkling merrily. 'I have a reputation for solving the most abstruse cryptograms, puzzles and conundrums, but I fear that this particular problem is beyond even my powers.'

'Say, Ollie, I have an idea.'

Mr Hardy's face bore a look of complete and utter amazement at this remark from Mr Laurel.

'You do?'

'Sure, I'm not as dumb as you look.'

'You certainly are not,' replied Mr Hardy, twiddling his bow tie. 'We will leave you in peace gentlemen. Come, Stanley.'

'Goodbye,' shouted Mr Laurel as they left.

'Good day to you both,' I called after them.

'Quick, Watson. There is not a moment to lose, we must run after them.'

I was most gratified to hear that Holmes had not been taken in by our visitors and had seen them for the madmen they were.

'If we are to overcome then, Holmes, shall I bring the police-whistle to attract the nearest bobby?'

'Overcome them? I have no intention of doing so nor asking the assistance of the police.'

'I do not understand. Then, why pray, we going after them at all?'

'Elementary, my dear fellow. I have not laughed like this for a long time. Come, Watson.'

Acknowledgements etc.

Thanks to The Galley Café in Lyme Regis for the coffee, chilli hot chocolate etc. I wrote some of this tale while relaxing there.

Thanks to Steve at MX Publishing.

Also to Bob at Staunch for another great cover.

Thanks to Gill for putting up with yet another Holmes tale and reading it through and offering suggestions.

If you haven't been to Venice. Please try....

Look out soon (and I know I say this often) for *Sherlock Holmes and the Scarborough Affair*. It will arrive....

David Ruffle Lyme Regis 2016

Also from MX Publishing

MX Publishing is the world's largest specialist Sherlock Holmes publisher, with over a hundred titles and fifty authors creating the latest in Sherlock Holmes fiction and non-fiction.

From traditional short stories and novels to travel guides and quiz books, MX Publishing cater for all Holmes fans.

The collection includes leading titles such as _Benedict Cumberbatch In Transition_ and _The Norwood Author_ which won the 2011 Howlett Award (Sherlock Holmes Book of the Year).

MX Publishing also has one of the largest communities of Holmes fans on Facebook with regular contributions from dozens of authors.

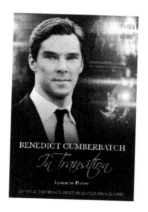

www.mxpublishing.com

Also from MX Publishing

Our bestselling short story collections 'Lost Stories of Sherlock Holmes', 'The Outstanding Mysteries of Sherlock Holmes', 'Untold Adventures of Sherlock Holmes' (and the sequel 'Studies in Legacy') and 'Sherlock Holmes in Pursuit'.

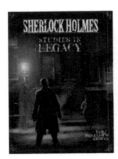 

The Amateur Executioner

London, 1920: Boston-bred Enoch Hale, working as a reporter for the Central Press Syndicate, arrives on the scene shortly after a music hall escape artist is found hanging from the ceiling in his dressing room. What at first appears to be a suicide turns out to be murder . . .

Lightning Source UK Ltd.
Milton Keynes UK
UKHW020005241118
332879UK00003B/80/P